Thoughts of Simon Drummond were farthest from Vicky's head until, coming back from her teabreak, she found him in the office with Sister Lorne.

'Simon, do you know Vicky, our new staff nurse?' Carole began, and then, catching the glance that passed between them, 'Oh! You do.'

Vicky scarcely heard her. For a moment it seemed that there was just herself and the registrar, and the flutter in her throat when their eyes met.

Dr Drummond broke the spell, a dimple flashing in his lean cheek. 'Yes, we have met. Hasn't she told you? She's my landlady, so I have to be nice to her or she may throw me out.'

'You mean—*this* is your globe-trotting spinster? Good heavens!' Carole broke into a peal of laughter. 'Simon! After all your grouses about absentee landladies, and she turns out to be one of us.'

Vicky grinned. 'Oh! Been maligning me behind my back, has he? And after all the creature comforts I left him.'

'We-ell, even *I* can't always be right,' the doctor admitted with an artless smile. 'The trouble is, it does rather complicate my immediate future.'

'I don't see why. Now she's back you could always share the place,' Carole put in impishly.

Grace Read has had a life-long love affair with nursing. Starting as a Red Cross Nurse in a London hospital during the war, she went on to do her general training in the Midlands. Marriage and a baby ended that career, but she retains a keen interest in the profession. She has a son and two daughters. Her youngest daughter is a nursing sister and keeps 'Mum' abreast of modern trends, vetting her novels for medical accuracy. When she is not writing Grace enjoys gardening, travelling to research backgrounds, and admits to a fondness for golden Labradors.

Dr Drummond Advises is Grace Read's eleventh Doctor Nurse Romance; recent titles include *Tides of the Heart, Casualties of Love* and *Call Dr Knight*.

DR DRUMMMOND ADVISES

BY

GRACE READ

MILLS & BOON LIMITED
ETON HOUSE 18-24 PARADISE ROAD
RICHMOND SURREY TW9 1SR

First published in Great Britain 1989
by Mills & Boon Limited

This edition 1989

ISBN 0 263 76352 8

Set in Palacio 10 on 12 pt.
03 – 8903 – 53563

Typeset in Great Britain by JCL Graphics, Bristol

Made and Printed in Great Britain.

CHAPTER ONE

AT THE END of her first week back at Wealdwood Hospital Staff Nurse Victoria Chalfont went off duty with a feeling of satisfaction. Yes, she had made the right decision in returning to England, and this lovely corner of Kent was just how she had remembered it in nostalgic moments during her self-imposed exile. In her mind's eye it was always high summer with wild roses in the hedgerows and banks of lacy cow parsley, and little leafy lanes leading nowhere in a hurry, and ancient church spires and conical oasthouses decorating the skyline. She had chosen to forget bleak Novembers—one bleak November in particular.

Wealdwood Hospital itself had seen a few changes in the two years since she'd been away. There was a newly-built Postgraduate Centre and an updated Accident and Emergency Department to cope with the ever-increasing demands on its services. The impressive Scanner Appeal sign which had sprouted by the main entrance signified even more ambitious projects ahead. But the countrified setting was still the same, with rising woodlands as a backcloth and pleasant lawns and flowerbeds surrounding the rambling buildings.

Making for the Nurses' Home—which was where

she was living for the time being—Vicky paused to admire a long bed of Masquerade roses in glowing sunburst colours. The border separated the road from a small parking area for doctors and VIPs. She might not have turned to see the sleek black Rolls Royce parked there had it not been for the two men who were talking by it.

One of the men she recognised—Ben Milden was an old friend from her previous days at Wealdwood. He was now the ENT registrar and she had already renewed acquaintance with him that week. His companion she didn't know—a scholarly but athletic-looking man with a wealth of darkly-blond hair, but it was his comment which had caught her attention.

'Beautiful, isn't she?' he'd remarked in a rich, deep voice, shapely head on one side as he stood back to take in the car's perfect symmetry.

As she followed his gaze, Vicky's tranquil mood gave way to the old, overwhelming sense of outrage. With difficulty she controlled an intense desire to throw things at the gleaming black beauty, but she couldn't resist muttering as she bounced by, 'It's not a *she,* it's just a heap of metal.'

The fair-haired stranger in the neat grey suit took a quick step after her and put a detaining hand on her shoulder. 'Hey, just a minute . . .' His eyebrows lifted a fraction, but there was a hint of a smile about his wide mouth. 'And who asked for your opinion anyway, Miss—er—V Chalfont?' he demanded, deep blue eyes straying to the name badge on her uniform dress.

His manner was one of amused tolerance while his

gaze took in the physical attributes of this cheeky young staff nurse who'd butted in on their conversation. Nice proportions, engaging heart-shaped face, but the brown eyes definitely hostile. And she practically tossed her silky dark hair when she spoke. All the same, he was unprepared for her angry rejoinder. It was beyond Vicky to treat it as a joke with that ghastly symbol of death confronting her.

'Well, it *is* just a heap of metal, isn't it?' she retorted, 'and as lethal as any other car on the road.'

'Dear me!' he murmured. 'Whatever brought that on?'

She met his searching gaze with an embarrassed half-smile, realising she should have had more self-control and kept her thoughts to herself. And she probably would have done had she not known Ben. Now, with cheeks growing hotter by the minute, all she wanted to do was to get away with as much dignity as possible. 'Sorry! You're right,' she admitted, switching her smile to include the quiet and inoffensive Dr Milden, 'it's none of my business what you choose to drool over.'

She would have walked on, but Ben coughed discreetly and his eyes twinkled behind his round, gold-rimmed glasses. 'Er—Vicky—I take it you don't know Simon Drummond? He's our senior paediatric reg, but he's been away since you came back. Vicky's going to be working on Coco Ward next week,' Ben went on by way of explanation to his companion.

For a moment her mouth fell open while her brain absorbed the information. Dr Drummond? *Dr*

Drummond? Ben thought he was merely introducing her to a man she was going to be working with. What he didn't know was that this might possibly also be the man who was renting her old home; unless there were two Dr Drummonds working at Wealdwood Hospital! 'Oh, er . . .' she stammered, 'no, we haven't met. Hello.'

'Hello!' Dr Drummond curbed a grin. 'Well, I promise I'll try not to rub you up the wrong way too often, if you'll promise me the same?'

'I don't normally have trouble getting on with people,' she returned lightly. It crossed her mind that she ought to say something about the house, but it didn't really seem the right moment, so she finished by giving a careless glance at the superb black motor car and saying, 'Is that thing yours, then?'

'Good heavens, no! But I can admire a superlative piece of engineering when I see it. Why does it ruffle your feathers, though?' he asked, his striking blue eyes watchful.

Involuntarily Vicky caught her bottom lip between her teeth, seeing again the slaughter outside the village Post Office on that cold November day over two years ago. It would have been simple to satisfy his curiosity, but she couldn't. She just *couldn't* put it all into words again, and to a stranger. Even now, when she thought she was so well adjusted. It was unnerving to find that she wasn't. Swallowing against the tightness in her throat, Vicky found a voice of sorts. 'Oh, it's nothing. Just a personal aversion I have. 'Bye for now.'

She walked on towards the Nurses' Home,

wanting to run but her legs feeling strangely inadequate. She could feel two pairs of eyes following her and guessed that Ben would be telling Dr Drummond something of past events. Oh well, it would save her the trouble of explanations later. But it would have been much better if she'd minded her own business and walked on by. For goodness' sake, if she was going to get paranoid every time she saw a big black car, people would think she was off her rocker!

Ben had been a Casualty Officer at the hospital at the time of the accident, so he knew the circumstances which had robbed her of mother, father and boyfriend in one swift blow. She had left the three of them sitting in her father's car while she called in at the local village store-cum-Post Office for some stamps. Nobody could have foreseen that a teenage boy, stealing a joyride in his father's new black Jaguar, would lose control and cause mayhem in the street. Her own beloved parents and Chris had died amongst the tangled wreckage. The boy himself, so she was told, had lingered on for weeks before they turned off the life-support machine.

Until the events which had shattered her world Vicky had been happy to live at home. It was convenient for the hospital and allowed her to see more of Chris. After the tragedy she had stayed with her aunt Celia and uncle Bob for a time. They had wanted her to move in permanently . . .

'Or at least until you've decided what you're going to do about the house, dear,' her mother's sister had said, 'because you won't want to live in the place all by yourself, will you?'

Until that moment the whole thing had had an air of unreality, like some hideous nightmare from which she would soon wake up. It was the remark about the house that shook her out of her stupor. It hadn't occurred to her that she needed to *do* anything about the house. Home was home. She still had that, didn't she, even if she'd lost the people in it. And it was a place where she could be herself, howl if she felt like it. At Aunt Celia's it was embarrassing when the talking stopped the moment Vicky entered the room and her uncle came out with one of his jovial guaranteed-to-cheer-her-up remarks. They were the kindest folks in the world, and she was grateful, but she couldn't settle there.

Neither could she find peace at her own home when she went back. Friends came to keep her company from time to time, but the memories which confronted her at every turn were too vivid for comfort. Finally, in desperation, she handed in her notice at the hospital, employed a reputable agent to let the house furnished, and took off for a fresh start at a hospital in Sydney.

For a time the new scene and the new friends she made there had worked well. Although she knew she could never forget, there was less anguish when she remembered. But links with her roots were not easily severed and sometimes she felt as though cutting herself adrift was, in a way, disloyal. In the end it was the necessity to do something about the house which had brought her back. There had been only one change of tenancy, and the agent had written to say that with the current contract shortly due to expire, the present tenant had asked would she be interested in selling it to him.

Vicky wasn't at all sure about that. The rent more than paid for the upkeep on the place and the modest mortgage which still existed. Besides, the thought of parting with it gave her a desperate need to see it again. After all, you couldn't grieve for ever. She might find she wanted to go back there to live after all. On the other hand, no single girl of twenty-four really needed a detached four-bedroomed house with two bathrooms and a sizeable garden. A labour-saving flat would be more sensible. But if the man she had just met should be the Dr Drummond who wanted to buy the house, that might make things rather awkward should she decide she wanted it back.

'Vict!' At the sound of her old abbreviated nickname Vicky snapped out of her reverie. She glanced up to see a tall, thinnish girl with spiky ash-blonde hair waving to her from an intersecting pathway, her angular features wreathed in smiles.

'Anna! *Hello*!' Vicky squealed in equal delight as the two girls hugged each other. 'I say, you've gone up in the world, haven't you?' she went on, eyeing the dark blue uniform which her old classmate now wore. '*Sister*, is it?'

'So would you be by now if you hadn't cleared off to the back of beyond. When did you get back?'

'Oh, just a couple of weeks ago, but I've only been working here a few days. Miss Alexander was very sweet about trying to fit me in. I'm a kind of holiday relief until she can place me permanently.'

'Well, you wouldn't have left, would you, but for that . . . awful accident to your folks. You living at the Ritz?' asked Anna, changing the subject and nodding in the direction of the Nurses' Home, a modern functional building of rosy brickwork with lines of identical flat square windows breaking up its flat square bulk.

'Yes, it was either that or move in with relatives, which I didn't particularly want to do,' Vicky said.

They walked on together, plying each other with questions, catching up with the past. At the time of Vicky's departure Anna herself had been away in the Midlands doing a post-graduate course in Neurology. 'So what really brought you back here?' she wanted to know. 'Didn't you like Aussieland?'

'Oh yes, I had a great time. But I was homesick for England and—well, really I've got to do something about my house . . .'

Anna looked incredulous as they pushed through the glass-panelled doors into the utilitarian entrance hall of the staff accommodation. 'You've still got your family house, and you're living *here*? If I could afford a deposit on somewhere of my own you wouldn't see me for dust!'

Explaining the situation, Vicky went on to conjecture that it seemed very likely that Simon Drummond might turn out to be the present tenant.

Her friend choked on a giggle, which had Vicky also seeing the funny side of it.

'Oh boy! I'd love to be a fly on the wall when you kick him out,' said Anna. 'Are you going to? Or are you going to sell it to him?'

'I don't know yet. The agent is supposed to be arranging a meeting between us, only he hadn't been able to get hold of the guy so far.'

Their rooms being at different ends of the building, the girls parted company after arranging to get together when their off-duty allowed. On reaching her own door Vicky found a telephone message scrawled on her memo pad hanging there. *Please ring your aunt Celia.* Going along to the communal phone in the corridor, she inserted her money and dialled the number.

'Oh, hello, dear,' Celia greeted her brightly. 'You got my message, then? I was beginning to wonder.'

'Yes, people are usually pretty good about passing on messages. Everything OK with you and the rest of the family?'

'Yes, fine. I really rang to tell you there was a call from that agent you've got your house with. He'd been able to contact the present tenant, who says he'll be there tomorrow afternoon or Sunday evening, and if you'd like to call round for a chat he'd be glad to see you, only would you please telephone first to let him know when.'

'Great—action at last!' said Vicky, sounding pleased although in fact she felt oddly apprehensive about the whole business. 'I'll be relieved to get it all sorted out one way or the other.'

'Well, that house is worth money, even if it does need a lick of paint here and there. Don't you let anyone talk you into letting it go for a song.'

'I won't . . . I'm not even sure that I want to sell

it—yet.'

'That's right, dear, you take your time. Although it probably would be the best thing to do. It you want some moral support when you go and see the man, your uncle or I could come with you. Anyway,' her aunt rattled on blithely, 'young Martin's Cub Group is having a barbecue to raise funds this evening. We wondered, if you're not doing anything, would you like to come? I'm sure he'd be pleased if you did, and its glorious weather for outdoor things, isn't it?'

Vicky smiled to herself. Ten-year-old Martin was the first of her cousin Claire's three children and Aunt Celia was a devoted grandmother. She was also determined to gather Vicky into their family circle, to be a substitute mother to her sister's orphaned child. Turning down the offer to make her home with them had taken considerable tact on Vicky's part, but having managed her own affairs for the past two years she had tasted independence and wanted to keep it that way. Aunt Celia was a dear and well-meaning, but she was inclined to take over if allowed.

Now Vicky said, 'That sounds like fun. Yes, I'd love to come. Thanks for asking me.'

'Oh, good!' Her aunt heaved a happy sigh, as at another objective achieved. 'Now, you'll stay the night, won't you? Your room's all ready. And perhaps tomorrow we could all do something nice together . . . take a picnic to the coast or somewhere. But we'll talk about that when we see you. Right, we'll pick you up tonight about seven. We'll be somewhere in that road opposite the hospital. OK?'

After saying goodbye to her aunt, Vicky thought

she ought to make an attempt to fix the suggested appointment with her tenant. Dialling the familiar figures of her old home number, she was suddenly conscious of her own heartbeat. It was banging away against her rib-cage like some imprisoned wild thing—which was ridiculous when all she was about to do was to make contact with someone about a business matter. In a way it was a kind of reprieve when there was no reply. Perhaps she did need a little more time to think things out. And there was no desperate hurry, was there? The tenancy still had another six weeks to run.

Going back to her own room, she took off her uniform, made herself a mug of coffee and relaxed on the bed in her bra and waist-slip. She tried not to think about the house, and the elusive Dr Drummond, and the Dr Drummond she *had* met—him with the clear blue eyes and the Nordic head and the voice with the resonance of a well-played cello. She concentrated instead on the watercolour of old Montmartrè which Chris had bought her on their last trip to Paris. She had hung it on the wall over the dressing-table as a reminder of happier times, but tonight it had lost the power to soothe her.

With a sigh of impatience she finished her drink, put on her white towelling bathrobe and flip-flops and padded along to one of the communal bathrooms to let a wallow in a scented bath soothe her instead.

Presently, cool and fragrant, she put on a bright cotton sun-dress, caught back the sides of her dark hair with a narrow primrose ribbon and fastened on a pair of gold pendant ear-rings. With the minimum of items packed into her overnight bag, she set off at a quarter to seven to meet her uncle and aunt.

Although Celia had said *about* seven, Vicky knew of old that this meant before and not after. Her aunt was early for everything—it was a standing joke in the family—so that she was not surprised to find the car already there waiting for her.

'We came a bit early,' her aunt explained, 'I need to pop in at Claire's on the way. I left my jacket there the other night and it's bound to turn cooler later. And I thought little Karen could come in our car . . . there's not much room in their Mini . . .'

Uncle Bob rolled his eyes and exchanged a patient grin with Vicky as he let her in to the back seat. 'Good job I'm the easy-going kind,' he said, which warranted a playful punch from his wife.

But there was to be no barbecue for Vicky or her relatives that night. On arriving at her cousin's small modern house on the outskirts of Tonbridge, they found everything in confusion. At least, more confusion than usual in that happy-go-lucky household (a rebellion against Claire's disciplined upbringing, so Vicky always concluded).

Tonight Martin's bicycle had been abandoned across the front path, the front door stood wide open and there were sounds of distress coming from the kitchen.

'Oh dear, whatever's the matter now?' Celia frowned, hurrying to find out.

Vicky followed her aunt into the house, expecting there to be a childish squabble over something or perhaps a grazed knee. She discovered her normally placid cousin fighting against tears while wringing out a cloth under the cold water tap, pleading anxiously with Martin to try and be brave. Dressed in his Cub's uniform, the lad sat on a stool whimpering piteously, one side of his cheek a raw mass, his eye rapidly closing, his nose bleeding.

'Oh God, am I glad to see you!' exclaimed Claire, greeting the startled visitors with heartfelt relief. 'He came a cropper off his bike—a lorry cut him up. I don't know what to do! He can't bear me to touch it . . .'

Aunt Celia was aghast and for once at a loss. 'Out of the way, you two!' she chivvied, moving aside the two gaping younger children to get a closer view. 'Oh dear! Vicky, you'd better deal with this . . . what's the best thing to do?'

It was evident to Vicky that this was more than a matter for simple home treatment. To her trained eyes the boy looked concussed, and his face would need thorough cleansing, a painful business. He would also need some antibiotic cover. Stooping to his level, she put her arms around him as she inspected the raw, grime-filled abrasions on his cheek and forehead.

'Ooh! I bet that hurts,' she said in a sympathetic voice. Taking a clean tissue from her own pocket, she gave it to him. 'There, you wipe your tears and dab your nose . . . I think it's stopped bleeding.'

To Claire she murmured, 'if you've got some Savlon, that's best . . . and some soft clean cloth. We'll mop up some of the dirt around the edges, than we can see how bad it really is.'

Her aunt shot off to find the Savlon almost before Vicky finished speaking and Claire produced some clean old rags. When she had done as much as she could without hurting the boy more than necessary, Vicky piled on the praise. 'My goodness, you're brave! I used to make a lot more fuss than that when I was a little girl and grazed my knees. All right, pet, that's all we'll do for now.' She made a big pad of a piece of old sheet. 'You hold this over the bad place and we'll take you along to my hospital. They've got some special cream there to make these sort of grazes better.'

With the two younger children left in charge of their grandparents, Claire drove to the A and E Department while Vicky cuddled up the scared youngster on the back seat. 'Isn't it lucky,' she told him, 'I know some of the doctors and nurses here because that's where I've been working this week, and they're all very kind, so don't you worry.'

In fact Vicky was pleased to find Sister Bonner on duty, a mature woman who had been nurtured in the old régime when everyone knew their place and student nurses minded their p's and q's. They still did when Sister Bonner was in charge. It was boasted she could run A and E singlehanded, and many a new houseman had cause to be grateful for her expertise. But she had a way with children and even the most difficult youngster became manageable in her hands.

Now, after a staff nurse had handed in Martin's particulars, she bustled towards them like a surrogate mother, and with a swift appraisal of his injuries, whisked him off to a cubicle to be seen by a casualty officer. 'Yes, Mummy, you come too,' she said pleasantly, when Claire hesitated.

Vicky stayed outside, talking to another of the staff nurses she knew, not wanting to seem pushy. Presently Sister Bonner reappeared and paused to give Vicky a brief résumé. 'It's a nasty graze, heavily contaminated. We'll be dressing it with Flamazine. I'm a bit concerned about his eye, though,' she went on. 'I'm going to see if I can get hold of Dr Drummond or Mr Lorne . . . they were both here not ten minutes since . . .' and she made off in the direction of her office.

In due course Simon Drummond himself came striding along the corridor, minus jacket, a bunched stethoscope protruding from the pocket of his well-cut trousers. He did a double-take when he saw Vicky in the waiting area. 'Hello!' he exclaimed. 'I met you earlier today, didn't I—Miss Chalfont?'

She smiled, a little surprised that he had recognised her out of uniform. 'Yes, you did.'

'Nothing wrong—with you, I hope?'

'No, I came with my cousin. It's her little boy you've been asked to look at. He had a fall from his bicycle.'

'Oh, I see. Right, I'd better do that.' With a brief nod he carried on towards Sister Bonner's office and presently they emerged together and disappeared behind the drawn curtains of Martin's cubicle.

While she waited Vicky watched the comings and goings in the department where she had been working until four-thirty that day. It had been an averagely busy session, although the load had thinned out by this time. Friday nights, however, were notoriously bad and she was glad they had hit a fairly quiet period. She was half relieved, half sorry that her stay in A and E had been short this time. True, it was terrific to be able to help in times of crisis, but there were also the heartbreaking occasions when all your efforts were in vain. Of course there would be the tragedies as well as the triumphs on the children's ward, which was her next assignment. On the whole, though, children were amazingly resilient and cheerful in the face of illness. It was their anxious parents who often needed the support.

Rapt in thought, Vicky was suddenly aware that Dr Drummond was now outside the cubicle and talking with the Casualty Officer. Eventually they went their separate ways and Simon Drummond came to have another word with her.

'We're popping young Martin into bed in Coco Ward when they've dealt with his face,' he explained. 'Keeping him under observation for a couple of days.'

'You're not unduly concerned, are you?' Vicky searched his face for reassurance.

His amazingly blue eyes met hers, and he smiled. 'Not unduly, but with head injuries one can't afford to be complacent. He's undoubtedly concussed. You can reassure his mother, though, that this is normal procedure for head injury.'

There was a certain curiousity in his continued unwavering gaze, his burnished head inclined in that characteristic way, as though he might be waiting for her to declare herself. But again it wasn't really the right moment for discussing private affairs, and she was glad when Sister Bonner claimed his attention on another matter.

Claire also had left the cubicle and came to join her. 'The nurses want to do whatever it is they have to do,' she said, 'and I seemed to be a bit in the way. Martin looks awful, poor kid. His eye is completely closed up now, and he's got to have an X-ray in case anything's broken. But he's being really good. I was quite proud of him, although it's the way they handle them, isn't it? That Dr Drummond's not bad, is he?' she chattered on in her usual imprecise fashion. 'Do you know him well?'

'No, hardly at all. I only met him today. *But,*' Vicky made a wry face, 'I have a sneaking suspicion he might be the man who's renting my house.'

Claire stared at her. 'Really? One way to find out—ask him!'

'I shall do, when I get the chance. I'll get round to it eventually. Now come on, how about a coffee while they're busy with Martin? They'll be a little while yet, then you can go with him when they take him to the ward. They'll let you see him into bed . . .'

They walked along the corridor to the coffee machine. 'Yes,' Claire agreed, 'they did ask if I wanted to stay the night, but I can't with Geoff being away. Anyway, Martin's not a baby—he knows I'll have to go home to look after the other two.' Now that she knew her son was in good hands she was less worried. 'I'm jolly glad you came around,' she said, 'or I don't know what we'd have done. I did wonder whether I should ring the doctor, but this time on a Friday night he wouldn't have been at the surgery . . .'

'No. Anyway, if ever you're worried and you can't get hold of a doctor, Casualty is the best place,' Vicky advised her.

'I suppose so. Gosh, I'm starving! A pity we missed out on the barbecue. Which reminds me, we ought to ring Mum or she'll be going spare. Oh, would you do that, Vicky? She'll bombard me with all sorts of questions which I can't answer . . .'

'OK,' Vicky laughed, and went off to put her aunt's mind at rest.

All plans for the weekend having come to nought, Vicky found herself being chief child-minder at her cousin's house for much of the time. It proved to be no mean feat in that small frenetic set-up. She rescued a box of matches from three-year-old Peter's busy fingers and stopped six-year-old Karen from eating a whole packet of chocolate laxative at one go. After which she went around the house putting a variety of lethal substances out of their reach and marvelling that all the children hadn't come to an untimely end long before this.

Not that Vicky wasn't glad to be of help, but she hadn't done any of the things she'd intended to do with her off-duty. Neither had she made that phone call to Dr Drummond by the time her uncle took her back to the Nurses' Home after tea on Sunday. Oh well, she would have to leave that for this weekend. After all, she could in truth claim there had been something of an emergency.

The evening, however, was still young, and with nothing better to do she could not resist taking a bus ride out to catch a glimpse of her old haunts again. She longed for a sight of the house which had been her home for all her formative years. The garden had been beautiful; she hoped it hadn't entirely gone to ruin.

The bus took her to the end of the quiet tree-lined road off the main street. It was all very much as she had remembered—detached houses of individual design sitting comfortably behind well-cut lawns, roses rampant everywhere, stately conifers, and flowering shrubs in profusion. Most of the properties seemed well kept up. She wondered if number twelve was going to look depressingly down-at-heel.

There were few people about and she met no one she knew. Walking on the opposite side of the road, she felt almost like an intruder come to spy out the land. As she neared her own property a middle-aged man turned out of his gate, walking a large white-coated dog on a lead. In the friendly way they had in those parts, the man gave her a pleasant 'good evening'.

Vicky paused to admire the dog's exquisite coat. 'He's gorgeous, isn't he? I don't know the breed. Is he a Chow?'

The man beamed, fondling his pet's head. 'No, he's a Samoyed. He's a lot of work to keep nice, but we're very proud of him.'

'Well, he's certainly a credit to you.' They stayed discussing the dog's merits for a few minutes, then the man glanced across the road and waved a hand to someone before walking on.

Vicky too glanced over, and the blood rushed to her cheeks when she saw Simon Drummond standing at the gate of number twelve. He was wearing workaday jeans, his broad chest bare and tanned, and he had apparently been cleaning out the red BMW which stood in the drive, doors open.

'Hello! You wanting me?' he called.

'I—um—er—yes and no,' Vicky returned, with an embarrassed smile.

Crooking a forefinger, he beckoned her over. 'You were supposed to telephone me first,' he said with a mild note of censure.

'Yes, I know. I have tried, but you're elusive.' She swallowed. 'Anyway, I was in the neighbourhood and I felt the urge to see the old place. I wasn't intending to call tonight. If it's inconvenient . . .'

'You'll have to take me as you find me,' he said, holding open the gate. 'Come along in.'

CHAPTER TWO

THE HEAVY oak front door stood ajar and Simon Drummond ushered Vicky into her own familiar entrance hall carpeted in the sage green Wilton that she and her mother had chosen together just six months before the accident.

'Sit yourself down in there while I find myself a shirt.' He pushed open the door to the lounge.

It was a curious feeling to be a visitor in her own home, and by permission of this blue-eyed stranger who had suddenly assumed a significant role in her private affairs as well as about to be part of her working life. Going into the long, graceful room with its diamond-latticed windows at one end and sliding patio doors at the other, she looked about her. The cottage-style chintz-covered easy chairs had worn well, so had the oatmeal carpet. The gilt-edged wall-mirror gleamed, and the coffee-table, bookcase and other items of furniture were dust-free. In fact everything spoke of the care of an industrious housewife, apart from a considerable amount of general clutter.

It did strike her that there were no pot plants or cut flowers, as in the old days. Her mother's collection of ornamental plates which Vicky had left on the walls was still there, but mementoes of her father's travels abroad which had decorated the natural stone mantelpiece had been replaced by a row of books between book-ends. Family photographs she had put away, together with other personal items, in locked cases in the loft.

She crossed to the open patio doors and looked around, breathing in the scents of the garden, delighted to find that it hadn't gone to ruin.

Simon Drummond returned, buttoning a clean fawn sports shirt across his broad chest, having exchanged jeans for tailored brown cords. 'That's better—now I feel civilised. Come and sit down, Miss Chalfont, and let's get things straight. You're the owner of this house, I take it. Right?'

She sank into the cushioned comfort of the nearest armchair and gave him her most winning smile. 'My name's Victoria, or Vicky, if you like. How long did it take you to twig who I was?'

'I wouldn't have had a clue, but for our little exchange in the car-park on Friday.' He sat opposite her across the room, one long leg propped upon the other taut thigh, studying her closely, so that after a moment she had to drop her gaze. He gave a slight smile and continued, 'I'd always imagined Miss Chalfont to be a mature lady of independent means letting the place while on her travels. I didn't know you were a nurse from Wealdwood, but when Ben told me that you'd just returned from Australia, well, it did seem a remarkable coincidence. And then there you were, skulking across the road . . .'

'Excuse me, I wasn't skulking,' Vicky interrupted indignantly. 'I wouldn't have come over if you hadn't seen me. My young cousin's accident kind of messed up my plans for this weekend. I thought I'd left it too late to phone you and make arrangements, but I just had the urge to come and see the old place.'

He clasped his hands behind the curve of his head, continuing to study her in a leisurely fashion. 'Yes, that's understandable. But why didn't you say something yesterday when we met in A and E?'

She shrugged. 'Why didn't you? Drummond's not exactly an unusual name. And I didn't know that *my* Dr Drummond worked at Wealdwood, did I?'

He laughed, a delicious infectious sound which made her laugh as well. '*My* Dr Drummond!' he repeated. 'I don't know that I like being acquisitioned. As a matter of fact, when I first took your house over I was at the County Hospital, not Wealdwood, so no, you wouldn't have known.'

To break the silence which followed she said: 'There were some things on the mantlepiece—a carved water buffalo, a Chinese vase, and a little jade figurine—what happened to those?'

'Oh, they're quite safe. I put them away in a cupboard, not wanting to be responsible for any breakages. You really shouldn't have left valuables loafing.'

'I know. It was rather silly, but I took off in a hurry. Thanks for taking care of everything—even the garden,' Vicky added, 'it's looking really beautiful. My parents were . . .' She paused mid-sentence and put a hand to her mouth as tears threatened. Oh God! She mustn't make a fool of herself, not in front of this poised, self-assured individual.

With nice timing Simon Drummond let his gaze wander in the direction of the open patio doors. 'Yes,' he murmured, 'it would have been a pity to let the garden go. It had obviously had a lot of t.l.c.'

His remarks gave her time to recover, and the use of the professional shorthand for 'tender loving care' brought a smile to her lips. She cleared her throat before going on: 'Do you do it yourself, or do you—have help?'

'No, to the first question. Yes, to the second. There's a nice lady who comes to clean for me and her husband helps in the garden.' He paused to control a smile. 'As to the question you *didn't* ask, I don't have a wife or a live-in lover, but my young brother Paul parks himself on me whenever he's at a loose end. He's at the Agricultural College. He's going to be awfully peeved if you kick me out at the end of my contract. And so shall I, for that matter. Have you thought about my offer to buy?'

'Well—er—no, I haven't, not yet.' Vicky fiddled with the gold chain around her neck. 'I haven't been back in England long, and I'm not sure of my plans.'

'Where are you living at the moment?' he wanted to know.

'At the Nurses' Home.'

'Oh! That makes me feel like a real cuckoo-in-the-nest, bedding down in comfort here while you make do with living in.'

Vicky laughed at his rueful expression. 'There's no reason why you should. You rented it, and it's yours until your contract expires. I'm the intruder.' She jumped up suddenly, thinking of something. 'Would you mind awfully, while I'm here, if I went up into the loft? I left some things in a case up there.'

'Sure. Go where you like, Vicky. I've never been up in the loft. Can you manage the ladder?'

'I always could. I used the place as a playroom when I was a kid.'

They both went out into the hall. 'I'll make coffee,' he said, 'but don't hurry.'

Running up the curving staircase to the broad landing above, she peeped into the bedrooms, hardly liking to go right in.

Apparently Simon himself was using the large front bedroom with its bathroom en suite. It was as one might expect to find with a normal man living on his own—a mess. His discarded jeans were slung across the bed, the duvet was where he had pushed it aside that morning, and the imprint of his head was still on the pillow. The dressing-table housed a jumble of brush and comb, wallet, cheque-book, loose change, wristwatch, pencil-torch, while the stool supported a pile of medical journals.

Young brother Paul seemed to have taken over the old guestroom. One of the twin beds was being used for its proper purpose, while the other acted as a receptacle for a variety of sports gear, including a wetsuit, surfboard, squash racket and hockey stick.

The fourth bedroom also had its share of surplus property, but her own room, amazingly, looked much as she had left it. Soft oyster-pink curtains at the lattice windows matched the dainty bedlinen. The padded bedhead in a darker shade of pink toned with the old rose carpet. White walls and fitted furniture completed the harmonious effect. It was a distinctly feminine room, and a slight fragrance in the air suggested it might have been used recently. Vicky wondered who had been sleeping there.

Pressing the button which operated the electronically-controlled trapdoor in the landing ceiling, she pulled on the cord and the loft-ladder obligingly came down. When she stepped up into the boarded and roomy loft her hand went automatically to the light switch on a rafter and the unshaded light-bulb cast its dusty glow over the relics of the past.

At the far end of the roof space was a door leading to the place which her father had used as a darkroom. The rest of the space with its cobwebbed dormer window had been an Aladdin's cave for Vicky and her young friends. Here amongst the discarded household brick-à-brac on wet days they had picnicked and played their games of make-believe. Now, after a cursory glance around, she found what she was looking for—the wicker workbox where she had left the suitcase keys. They were still there, undisturbed, ready to open the case in which she had packed family photographs along with some of her mother's personal treasures.

Perching on a discarded leather pouffe, Vicky took out a bulky brown-covered album which had been the last one in use. She began to glance through the colourful snapshots, mostly of happy, laughing people. There was her mother pruning the roses—her father stretched out in a deckchair—herself and Chris uncorking a bottle of champagne when they had celebrated his landing a job on leaving university. As she turned the pages her tears began to flow and before long she was weeping helplessly. She closed the book and buried her face in her hands, sobbing as she had not done since those early days when the accident had robbed her of parents and lover.

She wasn't aware that Simon Drummond had appeared in the hatchway to tell her that the coffee was ready. He heaved himself through and came to stand in front of her. 'You all right?'

Nodding, she blew her nose vigorously on her sodden handkerchief. 'Sorry. I—I will be . . . in a minute.' Then she shook her head as her tears refused to stop, clenching her fist and banging it angrily against the brown leather cover of the album. 'No! No! *No!* I—I'm *not* all right. What a d-damn stupid question!' she exploded between her sobs.

He squatted down in front of her, and he didn't offer sympathy, or say that he knew how she must be feeling. He just accepted the situation for what it was while passing her his own clean, dry handkerchief. 'Tell me about it.'

She shook her head again. 'I—I can't.'

'I think you should talk. If not to me, to someone,' he encouraged, his voice gentle. 'I gather from Ben you went through a very bad time a couple of years ago, and you bolted. But sooner or later reality has to be faced. It helps to grieve, Vicky. As a nurse, you should know that.'

Twisting his handkerchief into a ball, she bit her quivering lips. 'That textbook stuff's all very well—

in theory. I—it's not the same when it's you,' she blurted out rebelliously.

'Maybe not. Coming to terms with the death of *one* loved one must be hard enough to bear. It's not something I've had to face myself,' Simon went on after a pause, 'but I've known lots of people who have. They're all shattered for a time, some are angry, some fatalistic, some totally lost, but many people find reserves of strength they never knew they had.'

The dim lighting in the loft room made talking easier. Bit by bit he persuaded her to share her burden, the horror of the accident, the self-accusations afterwards. She told him she felt to blame, because if she hadn't wanted to stop at the Post Office for stamps at that particular moment her parents and Chris might still be alive.

Reasonably, he pointed out, 'And if an irresponsible youth hadn't chosen that particular time and place to go joyriding in a borrowed car it wouldn't have happened. You aren't to blame. It was the tragic consequence of someone else's stupidity.' He hesitated. For a moment he lifted his hand as if wanting to stroke her dark, bent head, but he ended by scratching his own cheek. 'Forgive me, Vicky, if I trot out that well-worn truism about accepting what you can't change and doing something about what you can.'

'Wh-what can *I* change?' she countered, between blowing her nose and sniffing.

'You can start by throwing out the guilt and making the most of your God-given self. You've got a lot going for you, compared with a great many people.' Rising to his feet, he reached down with his hands to help her up. 'Come on, go and clean up your face in the bathroom while I make us some fresh coffee.'

The touch of his hands seemed therapeutic. It was as though strength flowed from his fingers into hers. She wished very much that she could have gone into his arms, just to be held and comforted. But that, of course, would have been out of line.

Sitting opposite him in the lounge some few minutes later, hair combed, but red-eyed and denuded of make-up after sluicing her face with cold water, Vicky had to admit that she felt better for their talk, even if she did look a mess.

'How did you come here tonight?' Simon enquired, pouring her a mug of freshly-filtered coffee and passing the milk jug.

'By bus. When I lived here I always used to cycle to the hospital. Is my bike still in the garage? I might find that useful, if it hasn't fallen apart.'

'No, it's still in one piece as far as I'm aware—but scarcely roadworthy after all this time, I should imagine. Biscuit?' He pushed the plate of cookies towards her.

Absently Vicky took one, dunked it in her coffee and nibbled the warm, moist edge of it. 'No, I suppose not. Maybe I'll ask my uncle to pick it up and take it to the shop for me.'

'If there's no great hurry I could have a look at it for you,' he offered.

'Well, thanks, but there's no earthly reason why you should. I'm sure you've got lots to do with your time.'

His blue eyes twinkled. 'Never too busy to help a lady. It'll be a change from tinkering with my own lethal heap of metal!'

Vicky frowned. 'That's not funny, Dr Drummond.'

'Oh, come on, you'll have to grow a thicker skin. Anyway, it's not the cars which are lethal, it's the people who drive 'em. What about you, do you drive?'

'Yes, although I've never had a car of my own and I didn't drive in Australia.' Glancing at her wristwatch, she saw that it was after nine. 'I ought to get going or I shall miss the next bus.'

'Well, no need to worry about that. I'll take you back to the hospital. I was going anyway—there's a patient I need to check on.'

'Oh, thanks.' She relaxed and sighed deeply, half wishing that Dr Simon Drummond were not the decent man he appeared to be, so that when the time came she would have no qualms about telling him to leave. If she decided not to sell.

He was stretched out there in her father's usual chair, already looking as though he owned the place. 'You may think this is fanciful,' he confided, with a crooked smile, 'but ever since I came here it felt right, welcoming. People leave their aura behind them. I get the impression it was a happy place.'

'It was. I didn't appreciate my luck until it was too late. I took it all for granted,' Vicky mourned.

'Like most of us. Ah well, I can see you won't feel like talking business tonight. We'll arrange a proper date when you're more in the mood. That shouldn't be too difficult, now we each know who we are.' He levered himself out of his chair and eased his broad shoulders before crossing to close the patio doors. 'Shall we go?'

Vicky nodded agreement and presently, photograph album on her lap, she was sitting beside him in the red BMW, making the short journey back to the hospital. By tacit consent the vital issues were shelved for more general topics. She enquired after Martin and Simon told her that, all being well, the lad would be going home the following day. He asked about her experience with children and she told him she had been at a children's hospital in Sydney . . .

'That's why I asked Miss Alexander if she could find me a place on the Children's Unit here. I was in A and E before I left, but I wasn't too keen on all that trauma again, and I like Paeds . . .'

'At least that's one area of common ground we have,' he replied cheerfully, turning in past the hospital's Scanner Appeal sign and making for his special place in the medics' car-park. 'Are you working tomorrow?'

'Yes—on at one.'

'Then I shall most likely see you on the ward.'

They bade each other a polite goodnight. After leaving him Vicky was almost immediately joined by Anna, who was coming off a late.

'Hi, Vict!' said Anna, bubbling with curiosity. 'I saw you just get out of Drummond's car. So, were you right? Is it him who's got your house?'

Vicky smiled and said yes, it was.

'Well, come on, spill the beans! How did he react

when he learned who you were . . . and where'd you go to talk about it . . . and did you come to any decisions?' Anna paused, suddenly realising that her friend was not her usual lively self. 'Is everything all right, Vict? You look a bit fraught.'

'Oh, yes, everything's fine really, except I made a fool of myself. Of course, I had to go and delve into these old photos, didn't I?' said Vicky, tapping the album under her arm, after explaining how the doctor had come to invite her in, and how she felt about going back to the house. 'Looking through them, I started bawling—I couldn't help it. And Simon came and found me. He was very nice, though—talked to me like a Dutch uncle. It helped, but I felt such an idiot. And we didn't get to talk business at all . . .'

Anna linked her arm through Vicky's. 'Come and have a drink in my room. I expect he understood.'

Vicky smiled wryly. 'He probably saw it as a clinical exercise, encouraging me to get things off my chest, etcetera.'

'Well, you said it helped,' Anna reminded her. She made hot chocolate for them both, which she said would be better for them than coffee. 'More soporific. On a late I always bring the ward problems off with me. We had a motor-cyclist brought in today—only eighteen—fractured cervical spine and a depressed skull fracture. He's on a ventilator. It'll be a blessing if he doesn't make it, although I don't suppose his mum and dad will see it like that just now.'

'Oh dear!' Vicky sighed. 'And my only problem

is whether or not to sell a house! As Simon pointed out, compared with some people I don't know I'm born.'

'Is that what he said? What does he know about it?'

'Well, not in so many words, he didn't,' Vicky returned, 'but it's what he implied.' She sipped her drink. 'He's right, of course. People get wiped out every day, and life goes on, and we have to get on with it, and it's no good bearing grudges like me wanting to spit on every black car I see.'

Anna ran her fingers through her spiky fair hair, making it even more spiky. 'My goodness, he *did* give you a going-over! Maybe he had an ulterior motive. Perhaps he thought helping you let go the past would persuade you to sell him the house.'

'I shouldn't have thought that entered his head at the time. I think he genuinely wanted to help. I suppose I'd as soon sell it to him as anyone. But I don't know that I'm ready to part with it—not yet.' Vicky finished her drink. 'Oh well, wait and see.'

Anna laughed. 'Watch this space for a further thrilling instalment! Mind if I have a look through your photos?'

Together they browsed through the assortment of home and holiday snaps. Vicky found that she could look at them now with more detachment, even remembering the different occasions with a sad sort of pleasure.

'These are super,' Anna said. 'You should see some of my family's efforts. People either get decapitated, or cut off at the knees, or there's a thumb in front of the lens at the vital moment.'

'Oh well, you're seeing some of my dad's best here. He was something of an expert. The rest of us had our failures.' Vicky yawned hugely. 'I feel shattered, Annie. Must be your hot chocolate working. I think I'll call it a day, if you don't mind.'

'Yeah, me too. I'm on an early tomorrow. Where are you going to be working?'

'On Coco Ward. I'm hoping I'll stay on Paeds. What do you know about Sister Lorne?'

'Not a lot, except that she's married to our neuro consultant.'

Vicky frowned. 'I thought that was Sammy Seward?'

'No more, my child. He popped off with a coronary. It's Greville Lorne now. He's done very well for himself. *You* remember Grev—used to be the neuro reg when we were on nights.'

Raising her eyebrows, Vicky nodded, recalling the clever, rather solemn young man with a receding hairline and an unexpectedly dry wit. She had made him many a coffee while on duty in the small hours and they had got on rather well. She wasn't surprised to find him now at the top. 'I wondered why the name Lorne rang a bell,' she said.

Returning to her own room, Vicky felt all in, both physically and mentally. Tomorrow would be time enough to decide which photos to have framed for her dressing-table. Right now all she wanted to do was to sleep. Once she was in bed, though, her last conscious thoughts were not of faces from the past; they ranged around the touch of a strong pair of hands, and the sound of a rich deep voice telling her to go and wash her face while he made fresh coffee.

It was an odd sort of introduction to the senior paediatrician. She wondered what he had made of it after they parted. But since he had been en route for the children's unit to check up on a patient, doubtless that would drive such unimportant side issues right out of his mind. All the same, she was determined to be cheerful and enthusiastic on Coco Ward tomorrow. She couldn't have Simon Drummond—or anyone else for that matter—thinking she was a self-pitying drip.

And she really was looking forward to getting back to nursing children. Some nurses preferred the adult wards with their mostly compliant patients and the disciplined atmosphere. The chaotic informality of children's wards was not to everyone's taste, but Vicky found it fascinating. She especially loved the under-fives with their big, trusting eyes, who refused to be parted from their comfort blankets or battered teddies.

She had not yet seen Dr Drummond in action, but there was that humorous quirk to his curvy lips and a gleam of devilment in his wide-awake eyes that suggested a sense of fun. He would be good with the kids, she thought. All the same, there was a certain flintiness about the set of his jaw that suggested he was no soft touch. Simon Drummond would do what needed to be done and he would say what needed to be said without letting sentiment cloud the issue.

It was just a pity that *he* should be the one living in her house. What she had thought was going to be simply a question of deciding whether or not to sell was now going to be rather more difficult. She would have preferred to be dealing with a complete stranger so that there were no awkward pressures to bear on her decision. And she would much have preferred to start her new job without any undercurrents from the past to complicate it.

CHAPTER THREE

THE CHILDREN'S department was a single-storeyed addition to one side of the main hospital buildings and divided into medical and surgical wards. After lunch on Monday Vicky made her way to the surgical section with its colourful ward door painted to resemble a circus tent. Named Coco Ward after the illustrious clown and children's champion, it had the world of circus as its decorative theme.

Reaching up to release the high, child-secure handle, Vicky let herself into her new working domain with mixed feelings. On the one hand she was glad to be back in the familiar world of nursing children, which brought its own special challenges as well as rewards; on the other hand there were new workmates to meet, and Sister Lorne—married to the neuro consultant—was as yet an unknown quantity. Then, of course, there was the delicate situation between Simon Drummond and herself . . .

Hearing footsteps behind her Vicky paused to hold open the door for the tall, white-coated young doctor on her heels.

'Hello!' he said, following her into the cheerful chaos of youthful voices, swinging mobiles and bed-curtains bright with circus scenes. 'You new here? I don't remember seeing you around.'

She returned his friendly grin. 'Well, I'm not exactly new. I *did* work here up till two years ago, but I've been abroad.'

'Ah, that accounts for it. Whoops!' He paused while side-stepping an adventurous youngster who careered past them using an infusion stand as a scooter. Turning his attention back to Vicky, he went on ebulliently, 'Adrian Wood, Drummond's SHO.'

She introduced herself, her attention more on the activities in the ward than the talkative houseman. Nurses with coloured tabards over their uniforms were busy persuading children back to bed for their afternoon rest, while an auxiliary cleared away the remains of lunches and a play-leader tidied the toy-strewn playroom.

'Are you here permanently?' Adrian wanted to know.

'I'm hoping to be. At the moment I'm classed as holiday relief.' The ward door opened again to admit more nurses on the second shift. One of them greeted the SHO while others glanced at Vicky with some curiousity on their way to Sister's office. 'Well, if you'll excuse me,' Vicky smiled at him, 'I'd better go in for report . . . I haven't met Sister Lorne yet.'

'Oh, you'll like her. She's great.' Hands in the pockets of his white coat, he strolled along beside her and followed her into the Sister's office where the other nurses were now gathered. 'Carole, I just want to check on Baby Miller,' he breezed, 'OK?'

Sister Carole Lorne, small, vivacious and not looking a day over thirty, flashed him a dismissive smile and waved him away. 'Sure, go ahead. Nurse Baxter's giving him a small feed now. The last one stayed down.' She glanced towards the newcomer and the name-badge on her uniform. 'Nurse Chalfont—oh yes. You were doing paediatrics in Australia, Miss Alexander told me.'

Vicky nodded, well aware that the lively hazel eyes were rapidly sizing her up. 'Yes, I was at a children's hospital in Sydney.'

'Super. We must have a chat about that later. Well, this is June, Sarah and Marion,' the Sister said, introducing the rest of the late shift. 'What do you prefer to be called?'

'Vicky, please. Less of a mouthful than Victoria.' She smiled round at the other nurses, a third-year, a second-year and a mature enrolled nurse.

'Right. Pull up a chair and let's go through the Kardex.' Carole Lorne began a fairly lengthy report on each of their young patients, afterwards allotting specific children to the care of individual nurses. When they had dispersed to their duties she focused her attention on her new staff nurse. 'Thank goodness they've sent me someone with paediatric experience—they aren't too thick on the ground from the agencies. Come on, I'll show you the geography of the place while it's fairly quiet.'

Following the brisk, diminutive Sister out into the ward, Vicky said: 'There was a young cousin of mine in here yesterday. Martin West . . . has he been discharged yet?'

'Martin? Oh yes, his mother came for him this morning. Mild concussion—there was no fracture of the orbit, although his face looked a disaster, poor child. He'll be going to his own GP for dressings.'

She went on to point out the general layout of the department which comprised three six-bedded bays housing infants, toddlers and the over-fives. '. . . and as you can see, we have foldaway beds for any parent who wishes to stay. Then, these are the single cubicles for barrier nursing or very ill youngsters.' She nodded towards the only two occupied. 'That's Lisa, aged nine, osteomyelitis of the femur. The other is Baby Charles Miller, intussusception. He had a barium enema yesterday. We think it's possible that the enema may have straightened out the kink in his bowel, so he may not need surgery; at least for the time being.'

Vicky peered through the glass to where Adrian and Nurse Baxter were monitoring the four-months-old baby. 'Isn't his mum staying with him?' she asked.

'No. She's got four more at home, two of them under five, both with chickenpox. It can't be easy. We do have unrestricted visiting, of course.' Sister Lorne pushed open another door. 'This is the parents' rest-room where they can make drinks and relax.'

Looking in at the comfortably-furnished room with its pantry corner, Vicky smiled at a woman sitting having a cup of tea.

'Hello, Mrs Darby,' Sister Lorne said cheerfully, 'this is Staff Nurse Vicky. She was nursing in Australia until recently, so you two must have a chat some time.' She went on to explain that Mrs Darby was on holiday from Canberra . . . 'and they were just about to go home when Shaun had a fall and fractured his femur.'

'Oh dear!' Vicky put on a sympathetic face. 'How long ago was that?'

'Seven weeks now,' returned the mother with a tired smile. 'Dr Drummond says he'll be getting the splint off soon, then it'll just be a question of Shaun exercising his muscles. He's asleep at the moment, so I thought I'd go for a walk, get some fresh air. Unless there's anything I can do for you, Sister?'

Carole Lorne smiled at her. 'No, my dear. You have an afternoon off. Get yourself a nice lunch. Go into town and have a browse round the shops—it'll do you good. We'll keep Shaun amused and tell him where you are.'

Once outside Vicky asked, 'Is everything all right with Shaun?'

'It is now, but it was difficult for a time. He's asthmatic, and he developed a chest infection. I do feel sorry for his poor mother, though. Her husband had to go back to Canberra without them. Fortunately they were staying with relatives.' She paused as the SHO came out of Baby Charles's cubicle, leaving Beryl Baxter to settle the mewling infant. 'Well, Adrian?' she said.

He scratched in his longish, dark-brown hair, looking uncertain. 'We-ell, the bowel sounds are there all right, but it could be just a temporary improvement. What d'you think, Carole?'

'Time will tell. No point in making predictions at this stage. Will Simon be up later?' Sister Lorne asked. 'I shall need to know who can go home tomorrow and what we're expecting for Wednesday's list.'

'He was on his way to give a lecture to the School of Nursing last time I saw him, but he said he'd be back.'

The doctor and Sister went on to discuss other ward matters. Vicky stood trying to follow their conversation, but the mention of Simon Drummond brought him vividly to mind. She knew it was only a question of time before they met again, but how to handle it when they did was another matter. Her thoughts flew off into a string of what-ifs?—until Sister Lorne's well-bred voice called her back to the present.

'Vicky, when Beryl's finished with Baby Charles, you and she can do the drugs together. That will get you talking to all the patients, and any of the mums who are here.' She handed over the ward keys. 'I'm going for my lunch now. Any problems ask Beryl, or Marion. Oh, and fix yourself up with a tabard. They're in the linen cupboard.'

Thank you, Sister.' Vicky took the keys and went off in the direction of the service rooms. In the sluice she found June, the buxom third-year, testing a sample of urine. 'Hi! Where's the linen cupboard, please?' she asked pleasantly. 'This is all new since I was last here.'

'Just a jiff—I'll show you.' Washing her hands, June grinned. 'You don't remember me, do you?'

'Not really. Should I?'

'I was in Introductory Block when you were

staffing on A and E, and I had this crop of boils in my axilla which you dressed for me.'

Vicky laughed. 'Well, yes, I suppose you would remember something like that. I hope I treated you gently.'

'Oh yes. I was all starry-eyed about nursing then. I thought you were terrific!'

They walked along to the linen cupboard where Vicky chose a lavender tabard to put over her pale pink dress. 'Meaning you're not starry-eyed any more?' she queried.

'*That* state of affairs didn't survive my first spell of night duty, but I didn't fall by the wayside like some of my set. Finals next month.' June rolled her eyes in comic desperation.

'Yes, it soon comes along,' Vicky said, smiling. 'Well, you're getting all sorts of experience on this ward, so let's hope you get some questions on kids. Best of luck, anyway.'

'I'll need it! Well, better get back to my fluid charts.' June padded away on her black crêpe-soled lace-ups.

Having located where the drugs trolley was kept, Vicky waited for the staff nurse to be free. After introducing herself, she explained: 'Sister Lorne suggested I should come round with you—that way I can get to know everyone.'

Her friendly approach brought only a half-hearted response. 'Oh, all right,' said Beryl, with scant enthusiasm, and ran a weary hand through her ash-blonde shoulder-length hair.

'Nothing wrong, is there?' Vicky's warm brown

eyes were apprehensive. She hoped there was going to be no antagonism for whatever reason.

The other girl sighed. 'No! I've got a bit of a head, that's all. Better take something for it, I s'pose. 'Scuse me a sec.' She flitted gracefully off in the direction of the staff room, leaving Vicky to admire the girl's figure and thinking how nice it must be to be tall and elegant instead of an ordinary five-foot-four.'

In a few minutes the staff nurse was back and making apologetic noises. 'Sorry if you thought I was a bit off just now,' she said. 'It had nothing to do with you.'

'You had me worried for a moment!' Vicky patted her chest in relief, which brought the semblance of a smile to the other girl's lips.

'Just had a ding-dong with the SHO,' she explained, 'that's all.' Without further preamble Beryl opened up the drugs trolley and wheeled it out into the ward. 'Right, I'll dispense and you can check, OK?'

From then on they both became totally absorbed in the exacting and responsible task of giving the proper child-sized dose of the right medication to the right patients, as ordered on their prescription sheets.

Vicky cuddled and cajoled reluctant toddlers and chatted with the bigger children and made herself agreeable to their visitors. By the time the round was finished she had ceased to feel like a stranger and knew that she would have no problems in working with Beryl, who was efficient and painstaking.

The afternoon sped by, with the demanding world

of sick children calling for one hundred per cent vigilance on the part of the staff. The busy routine of treatments, bathing and feeding was constantly interrupted by the demands of the telephone, and there was always the need to spend time with a fractious bed-bound child or to read a story to a bored toddler. Thoughts of Simon Drummond were farthest from Vicky's head until, coming back from her tea-break, she found him in the office with Sister Lorne.

'Simon, do you know Vicky, our new staff nurse?' Carole began, and then, catching the glance that passed between them, 'Oh, you do!'

Vicky scarcely heard her. For a moment it seemed that there was just herself and the registrar, and the flutter in her throat when their eyes met.

Dr Drummond broke the spell, a dimple flashing in his lean cheek. 'Yes, we have met. Hasn't she told you? She's my landlady, so I have to be nice to her or she may throw me out.'

The Sister's eyes widened and her mouth gaped as she looked from one to the other. 'You mean—*this* is your globe-trotting spinster? Good heavens!' She broke into a peal of laughter. 'Simon! After all your grouses about absentee landladies, and she turns out to be one of us. I can't wait to tell Greville!'

For her part, Vicky would never have made their private business the subject of ward gossip, but since he had brought it up there was nothing she could do but go along with the joke. She grinned. 'Oh! Been maligning me behind my back, has he? And after all the creature comforts I left him!'

'We-ell, even *I* can't always be right,' the doctor admitted with an artless smile. 'The trouble is, it does rather complicate my immediate future.'

'I don't see why. Now she's back you could always share the place,' Carole put in impishly.

Simon clapped a hand to his forehead. 'Why didn't I think of that? Carole, my love, you're a genius!'

'Any time! Any little problems, just come to Auntie Carole.'

They both appeared to be fooling, it was true, but it made Vicky feel uncomfortable and her heart skipped a beat. Nevertheless, she decided to play it their way. 'I *might* have a few ideas of my own,' she returned flippantly.

Simon restrained a smile. 'That wouldn't surprise me in the least. Well, Carole, shall we get on with the work if you want me to clear a few beds for you?' He rose from his chair and looked into the ward. 'Now, where's Adrian got to?'

From the touch of impatience in his voice Vicky gathered that the registrar did not totally approve of his SHO.

'He's in the ward somewhere. Go and find him, will you, Vicky?' the Sister said. 'And I shall want you to do rounds with us since you'll be taking over when Beryl's off duty and I'm not here.'

Vicky eventually found Adrian in the ward kitchen, drinking tea with Beryl who looked a great deal happier than she had done earlier on. 'Adrian, sorry to interrupt, but Dr Drummond's asking for you. He's in the office,' Vicky told him.

He gulped the last of his tea, wiped his mouth with the back of his hand and bounced a kiss off Beryl's cheek. 'Thanks, petal. Duty calls. See you in the mess tonight, then.' Strolling back down the ward with Vicky, he gave her a cheeky grin and said: 'The same goes for you, if you're free, you know.'

'What does?'

'Drinkies in the mess? Come on, I thought you were an old hand.'

She laughed softly. 'Thanks, but I can't tonight. I've a load of things to do.' If there was something going on between those two, she had no wish to tread on Beryl's toes, especially after they had started off working so well together.

During the round Vicky was favourably impressed with Simon Drummond's approach to his young patients. He was friendly without being patronising and could coax a smile from the most peevish face. He also took time to answer questions from anxious parents, allaying fears where possible and wrapping up unpleasant truths in kindly words. Remembering how he had been with her the previous night, in her moment of despair in the attic, Vicky was not really surprised. But he would be no pushover if the occasion demanded firmness, of that she was in no doubt at all.

The last patient on his round was nine-year-old Lisa, the girl with osteomyelitis. The infection in her thigh-bone had not responded to antibiotics and her temperature remained erratic, her leg inflamed and painful.

In her single cubicle the wan-faced, dark-haired

youngster lay propped up against the backrest, a cradle taking the weight of the coverlet over her legs. A large Paddington Bear sat in the armchair beside her bed and the window opposite was plastered with get-well cards. Marion, her assigned nurse, had just finished making her clean and comfortable and was now engaged in threading a crewel needle with yellow wool for the tapestry which Lisa was attempting.

Having studied her blood tests and screened her latest X-rays in the office, Simon paused outside the cubicle and glanced at Adrian. 'Now, about this lass, the abscess has localised and I think it should be opened up and drained as soon as possible. Agreed?'

Adrain nodded. 'The systemic drugs don't seem to be getting there, do they?'

'I did warn her mother that surgery might be necessary,' Simon went on, 'but has she said anything to Lisa, does anyone know?'

'Not that I'm aware of ,' Carole returned.

The registrar stroked his chin thoughtfully, then he smiled at the child through the glass, waved to her and moved on. 'We'd best not mention it until her mother comes. And we shall need Mrs Kemp to sign the consent form. What time does she usually get here?'

'Between six and seven as a rule,' the Sister said. 'She comes after work, except at weekends.'

After a general discussion it was decided that since Vicky would be the nurse in charge when the early shift went off duty, she would let Simon know when Lisa's mother arrived. 'You can tell her I want to see her—explain what it's about without alarming her. Parents sometimes find it easier to talk to nurses than to doctors.' He smiled at her. 'You'll do that, will you?'

'Yes, OK,' said Vicky. It wasn't the first time she'd had to prepare people for what was to come, and it wasn't that which caused her pulse to quicken. It was something about those deep blue eyes looking steadily into hers. She hoped her rising colour wasn't obvious to the rest of the group.

Handing over before she went off duty, Sister Lorne reminded Vicky of the things to be done that evening. 'Keiran's to have his stitches out and he can go home tomorrow. So can the two tonsillectomies, Dana and Kevin. And remember Dr Drummond wants to see Mrs Kemp about the consent for Lisa's surgery.' She took her stylish Gucci shoulder bag from the cupboard. 'You shouldn't have any problems. I'm off to the ballet tonight—if my benighted husband can tear himself away from his precious patients! I'm going to rout him out now. 'Bye.' Flashing her new staff nurse a brilliant smile, she was gone with the rest of the early shift.

In the middle of children's suppers the ward was alerted to expect a road traffic accident victim. Vicky took the message. 'It's a girl of about five, right parietal skull fracture. She's going to theatre for debridement of wounds,' she told Marion who was in the kitchen making up a feed for Baby Charles. 'They don't know who she is yet. She was picked up among the flowers by the side of the motorway, so they've called her Daisy.'

'Why—what about her parents?' the middle-aged nurse asked, her round kindly face creased with concern.

Vicky shrugged. 'Bit of a mystery. The woman in the car they believe she came from was also unconscious. She'll be going to ITU. The police are checking on addresses in her handbag.'

Marion sighed. 'Someone's in for a nasty shock. I can remember how it felt the time a policeman came to my door after my son came off his motorbike.'

'Oh,' Vicky almost hesitated to enquire. 'Was he—badly injured?'

'Fractured femur. Fortunately he's got himself four wheels since those days. A bit less risky than those awful machines, but only just, the way he drives it. Boys!' said Marion with a despairing shake of the head.

'Well, this child'll have to go in that cubicle next to Lisa. She'll need specialling, won't she?' mused Vicky. 'You've got enough to do . . . it'll have to be June.'

'With a bit of luck perhaps she won't be up till the night staff come on. Thank goodness for a few reliable mums like Mrs Darby to help out!'

Marion went off to give the baby his feed while Vicky prepared the cubicle ready to receive their new patient. On a children's ward there were never enough hands to go round and always the unexpected happening to hold things up. But somehow the work got done.

Later, on seeing Lisa's mother with her, Vicky

bleeped Dr Drummond as requested.

'Well, I'm very involved here for the moment,' he returned. 'If I can't get up before she leaves ask her if she'd mind coming along to Casualty, will you? They'll find me. Have you told her what it's about?'

'No, not yet. But I will.'

'Fine,' he said, and rang off.

Putting down the phone, Vicky was wondering when best to approach Lisa's mother when Mrs Kemp came to the office with some fruit yoghourts for her daughter. 'I brought these for Lisa,' she said. 'They'd better go in your fridge, hadn't they, Nurse?'

'Yes,' Vicky smiled at her, 'I'll put her name on them. Mrs Kemp, will you sit down a moment?' She patted the chair beside her.

The woman seated herself, looking anxious. 'Lisa's no better, is she? Is that what you want to tell me?'

'The infection isn't responding to the antibiotics as well as Dr Drummond had hoped,' Vicky replied gently. 'The problem is, the abscess is deep in the bone. She needs to have it opened up to let the pus out, and that will require a trip to theatre and a general anaesthetic. Dr Drummond said he did mention that surgery might be necessary.'

'Oh dear!' Mrs Kemp murmured. 'Yes, he did say something about it.' Her chin began to tremble, 'Tell me honestly, Nurse—I mean, it's not cancer, is it? She won't lose her leg?'

'No, it's not cancer.' Vicky shook her head, glad to be able to reassure the mother. 'Osteomyelitis is a serious infection, but it can be cured with modern drugs. Once the abscess is drained, then Lisa should improve rapidly.'

'Oh, thank God for that!' The mother fumbled in the pocket of her linen jacket, found a tissue and blew her nose. 'She's all I've got, you know. Her father left us when she was two.'

Vicky reached over and laid a hand on the woman's shoulder. 'Try not to worry,' she said. 'With surgery they'll be able to put the penicillin right where it's needed, which is the most satisfactory way.'

'When do they want to do it?' Mrs Kemp asked.

'Dr Drummond would like to talk to you about that. He'll need your signature on the consent form before he can go ahead. He did say he'd try to get up to the ward tonight, but if he hasn't managed it before you leave, would you mind calling in to see him at Casualty on your way out? He'll explain everything then.'

'Yes, of course. Er . . . what about Lisa . . . does she know?'

'Not yet. Shall I come with you to talk about it? She's a sensible little girl, isn't she? Very bright for her age.'

The woman smiled and nodded. 'Yes, she's got her head screwed on all right, has Lisa. I expect she'll take it OK—better than me, probably. I'm a terrible coward—I even hate taking her to the dentist!'

Vicky smiled as they walked together towards Lisa's cubicle. 'Children are always amazing me. Often they're much braver than the rest of us.'

Lisa did, in fact, take the news quite indifferently.

'Anything'll be better than lying here with my leg feeling hot and hurty all the time.' She thought for a moment, then added, 'Will it be like you see on telly—all those people standing round in masks, and me in the middle?'

'Something like that,' Vicky nodded, 'but you won't know anything about it. You'll be fast asleep.'

'They will make really sure I'm asleep before they do anything, won't they?' the little girl asked, with a hint of anxiety.

'You bet they will! Before you know it you'll be back here in bed and it'll all be over. Dr Simon will look after you.'

'Yeah,' Lisa said with a shy smile. 'I like him.'

Her mother rolled her eyes and laughed. 'Good thing she's not a few years older, that's all I can say! Well, I ought to be going. Shall I pop down and see him now?'

'Yes, if you wouldn't mind,' Vicky said. 'Tell someone in charge he's asked for you, and they'll find him.'

It was eight-thirty and the night staff were just arriving before the unidentified road accident victim was brought to the ward.

Vicky directed the theatre porter to the prepared cubicle and arranged the covers over the limp little form of 'Daisy' when she had been transferred from trolley to bed. 'Just debridement of scalp wounds, was it?' she asked the recovery nurse, gazing down to the child's bruised face and the flaxen curls fringing her bandaged head.

'Yes—Mr Lorne wants full neurological obs and a fifteen-minute pulse check. It was a hundred and thirty when I last took it, and her pupils were equal and reacting,' the theatre nurse reported. 'Still no news as to who she is, poor kid.' She handed over the case notes and advised that the doctors would be up shortly.

Vicky checked and recorded the child's vital signs, satisfied herself that the intravenous infusion was flowing correctly, and put up the cot sides. She then briefed June to keep watch while she herself went to give her report to the night staff.

In due time both the neurological consultant and Simon Drummond arrived to check on the welfare of the new patient. Greville Lorne's eyebrows lifted when he saw Vicky. 'Hello! Where did you spring from?' he exclaimed.

She grinned at him. 'Australia.'

'Oh, really? Some spring! Well, good to see you again, Vicky. So I assume you've already met my dear wife?'

'Yes. I thought she was taking you to the ballet tonight?' Vicky recalled with a slow smile.

He made a comic face. 'Saved by the call of duty! Carole wasn't too pleased, but she found a friend to go with her instead. The joys of being married to a surgeon. How's little Daisy?'

Vicky took them to the cubicle, where June reported no responses, but pupils still equal and reacting.

'Pulse and blood pressure OK?' said Greville,

studying the graph. 'Fine. Keep the observations going and report immediately any fall in pulse rate or rise in b.p.' He glanced at his wristwatch and sighed as he ran a hand over his receding brown hair. 'Well, I did promise to meet Carole for dinner afterwards, if possible, so I'd better shoot. You'll be about, Simon, to keep an eye on this lass for a time?'

The registrar nodded. 'Yes, I shan't be far away.'

'I'll say goodnight, then.' Greyille Lorne beamed at Vicky. 'I must get Carole to arrange a dinner party to welcome your return to the fold.'

When the neuro-surgeon had left, Simon parked himself in the office and brought his case notes up to date. Vicky got on with her own interrupted duties, flying about making sure that all was in order before handing over to the night nurses.

The registrar caught her up at the ward door as she was about to leave. 'Well, what's the verdict on your first day on Coco?' he asked.

'Great!' she said. 'They're a good crowd.'

Looking down at her from his superior height, he smiled as they walked along the corridor together. 'Work, that's the best tonic, isn't it? Where are you off to now?'

'Back to my four walls and a belated beans on toast.'

'Ouch! You're making me feel like a squatter again.'

She laughed softly. 'Don't be silly.'

'Come on, I'll treat you to a meal at the Black Swan. Their fodder isn't at all bad.'

The invitation was tempting. Simon Drummond

was undeniably fascinating company, but something told Vicky it might be wiser to avoid socialising, at least until she had decided what to do about the house. She hesitated, looked down at her uniform dress and made that the excuse. 'Thanks, but I'm not dressed for eating out.'

'Then slip back to your room and get into a pair of jeans or something. It won't take you a minute. I promise not even to mention houses—although,' his lips twitched humorously, 'that wasn't a bad idea of Carole's.'

She looked at him uncertainly. 'You mean—about sharing? You're not serious!'

He merely laughed, holding the door for her as they left the hospital. 'Go and get changed. I'll see you over there in about ten minutes, eh?'

It would have seemed ungracious to refuse. After all, he was probably only trying to be helpful, knowing what he did about her. She shrugged and smiled and said, 'OK, I'll get my skates on.'

But hurrying back to her room, she didn't quite know what to make of this man. Was he teasing about sharing the house? That deep-throated laugh had been no answer at all.

CHAPTER FOUR

BACK in her room Vicky changed out of uniform as quickly as possible, pausing only for a quick wash to freshen up. After all, he'd said jeans and ten minutes, and she wasn't out to impress him, was she? It made for easier relations to keep things on a casual basis.

She put on the first things to hand—a straight denim skirt and a primrose cotton-knit top which was cool and comfortable. Bare legs and her strappy summer sandals. Apart from a bit of lip-gloss, she didn't even bother with make-up—her skin still had a flattering golden tan from her days in Australia anyway. But combing through her dark silky hair, Vicky felt nothing like as composed as her reflection in the mirror suggested.

It was just a short walk from the hospital grounds to the Black Swan, a picturesque seventeenth-century inn, its red-tiled roofs at crazy angles. On this warm summer night customers sat eating and drinking at tables in the garden while others lingered on the patio enjoying the exceptionally fine weather. Even at almost ten o'clock the atmosphere was balmy.

Pink-cheeked and a little breathless, Vicky made for the low-ceilinged twisty-beamed saloon bar where Simon had said he would meet her. Looking round for his distinctive burnished head, she saw him perched on one of the high padded stools at the counter, and she couldn't have been more pleased to see Ben Milden sitting with him. Ben had always been one of her favourite people; besides, having a third person there would be bound to make conversation easier.

Working with Simon had presented no problems, but meeting him socially on her own was a different matter. She felt she couldn't have made the best of first impressions. Their brush in the car-park, for instance, then her arrival unannounced at the house, and her weeping session in the attic. Goodness knows what he must think of her.

Going over to join the doctors, Vicky said merrily: 'Hi! Didn't I do well?'

Simon slid off his stool, consulted his wristwatch and raised an eyebrow. 'Not bad. I wondered if you'd change your mind.'

'Would I have dared?' she challenged with a grin.

He shot her a discerning glance from under his straight brows. 'Yes, I think you might. Don't you, Ben?'

The ENT registrar smiled his quiet smile and said, 'I'm glad she didn't. She improves the scenery. Have a seat, Vicky.' He moved a stool so that she could sit between them.

'What will you drink?' Simon asked.

'Oh, something long, please. Cider would be nice.'

Ordering it, Simon also asked for the menu. 'Ben's going to join us for something to eat. And he can act as referee if I tread on your toes again, can't he?'

She let that pass and turned to smile at Ben. 'Fine! We're old friends, aren't we?'

'Yes. At least, I thought so, until you decided to disappear without so much as a goodbye,' he returned mildly.

'Oh well, you know how it is,' Vicky shrugged, 'you were probably missing at the time . . .'

The barman interrupted with requests for their orders. They decided to eat in the garden, and despite her original misgivings it turned out to be one of the best evenings that Vicky had spent in a long time. There was no awkwardness, no under-currents—at least not noticeably so. The converation ranged back and forth in a lighthearted manner during their alfresco meal under the night sky. Vicky caught up on what had happened to whom, and was in turn asked about her experiences in Australia.

'I suppose eating out is no novelty for you now,' Simon remarked with forkful of moussaka poised. 'They do it all the time, don't they?'

'Mmm—lots of barbies and picnics. But I missed the changing seasons. Christmas dinner on the beach with the temperature in the nineties doesn't seem quite right somehow . . .' It suddenly occurred to her that she was doing a lot of talking, prompted by questions from her companions, and that Simon's thoughtful blue eyes seemed intent on committing her to memory. She stopped short and laughed. 'OK, enough about me. Have either of you ever worked abroad?'

Ben said only if you counted Jersey as abroad. Simon said that he'd spent a year in Toronto but had been glad to come back. 'They don't play cricket out there,' he complained.

Vicky laughed. 'Then you should have gone to Australia—or even Pakistan, perhaps.'

'No, thanks. I had my fill of foreign parts as a kid. My father was based in Karachi—that's where I grew up until I was seven. Then I was sent back home to boarding school.'

'Oh, poor you!' Vicky's lively imagination conjured what it must be like to be packed off to school at a tender age, far away from your nearest and dearest.

'I didn't mind all that much,' Simon returned. 'I used to spend rattling good holidays with my aunt Lavinia, in Tunbridge Wells, actually. She was terrific—spoiled me like mad.'

'She's the lady whose nasal polyp I removed,' Ben remembered. 'Quite a character, isn't she? Invited me to go and see her collection of model soldiers, but I never have.'

'You should,' returned Simon. 'She'd be delighted to show you her treasures. The house is a real museum piece and the garden's a gem—wild, mind you, but beautiful.'

As closing time approached tables were emptying and a waitress came round with a tray, gathering up empty plates and glasses. 'I think it's time we went,' Vicky said. 'It's been great, though. Thanks for a lovely meal.'

Ben had his car on the pub forecourt, but Simon had left his at the hospital. 'I need to look in on the ward anyway,' he said.

After waving goodbye to Ben, Simon and Vicky turned in the direction of the lighted hospital buildings where the hum of activity never ceased.

Being alone with him, and at this late hour, was not as easy as it had been with Ben's stabilising influence at hand. Vicky felt oddly nervous with Simon strolling along beside her, their bodies within touching distance. She found his physical presence disturbing; there was a kind of chemistry which caused her blood to tingle. Not even Chris—whom she had loved—had affected her in quite this way. Time she took a firm hold of herself; it wouldn't do to let the man run rings around her.

Taking refuge in the subject of work, Vicky swallowed and said, 'Oh, I meant to ask . . . did Lisa's mother manage to find you, to get the consent form signed?'

'Yes, everything's OK.' Even his rich, melodious voice sent a quiver down her spine. 'We're fitting her in tomorrow afternoon. It appears your explanations reassured Mrs Kemp that we're doing the right thing.'

'Oh, good. Everyone's happy, then.'

'We-ell, that's debatable.' Pausing at the entrance to the Nurses' Home, Simon studied her with a crooked half-smile. 'I kept my promise tonight, didn't I?'

'What promise?' she asked, although she guessed what he meant.

'Not to talk houses.'

'Oh, that.' She smiled. 'We couldn't very well, not with Ben being there.'

'Maybe not. But we shall have to, shan't we? I'll give you a little more time to get settled, then we must make a date to thrash things out. Well, goodnight, Miss Victoria Chalfont. I must say you're not a bit like the lady I'd imagined.' He grinned at her and was gone.

Returning to her own plain but functional room, Vicky sighed, the pleasure of the evening somewhat marred. Blow you, Simon Drummond, I wish you'd settled in someone else's house, she thought resentfully. Now here he was, urging her to make decisions which she wasn't quite ready to make.

In the end she supposed she'd have to sell him the place if he wanted it. After all, he had looked after it. Then there'd be the complicated business of sorting out the proper market price, and what to charge for the furniture and fittings if he wanted those as well. He'd said he didn't have a wife or a live-in lover, but that didn't mean there wasn't a girl in his life, and a girl might want it furnished to her own taste.

Of course it was foolish and impractical of her to think of living there herself. She'd tried that, hadn't she? Forgetting sentiment, if she sold it she'd have the money to pay off the mortgage, and enough left over to buy a flat. Perhaps Anna might be interested to share with her?

Too mixed-up to think about it any more that night, she decided to shelve the matter for the time being. Why not let things run their course and see what happened? Which was not an attitude her aunt Celia would have approved of, Vicky thought wryly.

Aunt Celia liked all the i's dotted and the t's crossed. And that brought another thought to her head. Oh dear! She really should have enquired how young Martin was getting on. She must remember to do that tomorrow.

Her last conscious thought was that Simon himself would probably have preferred to be dealing with someone else. Better his imagined elderly spinster than a woolly-minded staff nurse who didn't know what she wanted. In all fairness it was time she made up her mind one way or the other.

Going on duty at seven-thirty the following morning, Vicky was glad to find that their road accident victim of the previous day had recovered consciousness and her condition was satisfactory.

'. . . and would you believe it, her name really is Daisy?' Staff Hazel Fisher reported. 'How's that for a coincidence! The girl driving the car was her nanny, not her mum. The parents were out for the evening. Her mother's with her now, though. Daisy's still drowsy, but rousable, and we're keeping her on hourly obs until further notice.'

More good news was that Baby Charles had kept his feeds down and his last nappy change had been satisfactory. And Lisa's father had telephoned and said he would be coming in to visit her.

With the rest of the report given and duties assigned, Vicky went along to check on Daisy and greet the mother.

'Good morning, Mrs Gates,' she smiled, and bent to look at the child who lay curled on her side, eyes closed. 'Daisy gone to sleep again, has she?'

Mrs Gates, a young woman of about thirty, still wearing the filmy black party dress of the night before, nodded, the signs of strain evident in the dark circles under her eyes. 'Yes, she just seems to want to sleep, Nurse.'

'But she knows you all right? She's recognised you?'

The mother gave a heartfelt sigh. 'Yes, thank God. And all her limbs seem to be working properly. I can't believe how lucky we are! They say Rachel's going to be OK, too—that's her nanny, who was driving. Apparently the car's a write-off. It's a miracle . . .' She buried her face in her hands and shuddered.

'Yes, miracles do happen sometimes,' returned Vicky gently. 'What time did you find out about the accident?'

'I got home about two a.m. The police had called on my neighbours, and they'd put a note through the door. Her father doesn't know yet . . . he's away on a business trip. I—I don't know how I'd have told him if . . . I mean, he's not too keen on the social demands of my job, anyway.'

Vicky put a comforting arm around the woman's shoulders. 'Daisy will be all right in a day or two . . . rest and quiet works wonders. And how about you? Have you been sitting here all night? Come along to the rest-room and close your eyes for a while. I'll organise you some breakfast presently . . . we'll call you if Daisy needs you.'

* * *

The rest of the day continued its satisfactory pattern. That morning, when the doctors came round, with Shaun's X-rays showing complete healing of his fractured femur, his Thomas's splint and skin traction were removed. Much to the seven-year-old's disgust he was not able to leap immediately out of bed.

His mother laughed. 'He thought he'd be getting up straight away,' she said, watching Simon putting the boy through a few limited movements.

'All in good time. This leg isn't as strong as your good one yet, Shaun,' Simon cautioned. 'It's going to feel wobbly when you first put it to the ground, but do your exercises and you'll soon be hopping on the plane home again to see your dad.'

On leaving Shaun's bedside, Vicky accompanied the two doctors to Lisa's room, where they studied her charts and looked at her leg.

'Well, young lady,' Simon smiled at the child, helping to put back the protective cradle and bedcovers, 'time we did something about making this leg better for you, isn't it?' He sat down on the chair beside her and replaced one of her Paddington Bear's boots which had fallen off. 'I saw your mummy last night and she thinks so too. So we'll give you some sleepy medicine presently and see what we can do, OK?'

Lisa nodded, her eyes large in her trusting face. 'Except . . . my daddy's coming to see me . . . he phoned to say he was. And I don't want to be asleep when he comes . . .'

Simon straightened Paddington Bear's black felt

hat. 'Yes, I heard he's phoned—that's super, isn't it? If you *should* happen to be asleep when he comes, I expect he'll want to stay until you wake up.' He sat the bear in the bed beside her and gently stroked her dark hair. 'See you later, then, Lisa.'

Leaving the cubicle, he handed the notes back to Vicky. 'It'll be barrier nursing after we've opened this leg,' he reminded her.

'Yes, naturally.' She was surprised that he should have thought it necessary to mention it. 'I didn't explain that to her mother yesterday, but I will, or I'll make sure that someone does. I thought she'd had enough to take in at the time.'

'Fair enough,' Simon returned. 'We just don't want the parents alarmed unnecessarily, do we? I hope the father keeps his word.'

Adrian draped an arm around Vicky's shoulders as they moved to check on the patients for discharge. 'What's all this carry-on about Lisa's father?' he queried.

Simon scowled at him—or, more precisely, in the direction of the arm which had now slipped to Vicky's slender waist. 'You've read the domestic history—in fact, you wrote it, as far as I recall,' he said brusquely.

'What? Oh yes, divorced, aren't they?' Adrian remembered. 'I suppose she doesn't see much of him.'

In the office the telephone was ringing, which gave Vicky the chance to escape from Adrian's hold. From the registrar's frosty manner she gathered that he objected to his SHO's nonchalant attitude. Either that, or he disliked familiarity on the ward.

'It's for you, Simon,' she said, returning.

Watching the registrar's tall, straight figure make strides towards the office, Adrian murmured, 'What's biting him?'

'Busy night, perhaps?' Vicky suggested.

He laughed, 'So what's new?' and looked at her with a provocative grin. 'I only had four hours' sleep last night, but I could promise to stay awake if you'd like to have a drink with me this evening.'

She also laughed, but shook her head. 'Thanks. Nice of you to ask me, but I don't poach on other people's preserves.'

He looked puzzled, then said, 'Oh! Meaning Beryl? We're just good friends, you know.'

Simon returning put an end to that conversation and the two doctors went off together.

Sister Lorne came on duty at one o'clock with the rest of the late shift. After Vicky had given them a résumé of the morning's activities, she stayed to ask the Sister how she'd enjoyed her evening out. 'What a pity your husband couldn't make it,' she said.

Carole Lorne wrinkled her pert nose. 'That's life! At least, it is if you're married to someone as dedicated as Greville. Well, he missed a treat, but my friend enjoyed it. They put a Big Top up in the grounds of Leeds Castle—wonderful setting, ideal for *Swan Lake*. It was absolutely terrific.' She eyed Vicky enquiringly. 'You've worked with my husband before, he told me.'

'Yes. He was registrar here when I did my time on Neuro. It was nice to meet him again.'

'Yes, small world!' Carole said.

Vicky went off to her own lunch, meeting Anna in the canteen, who gave her news about Rachel, Daisy's nanny.

'It seems she'd just collected Daisy from a birthday party. On the bypass her windscreen was shattered when a lorry in front of her shed its load of oil drums and all hell broke loose. She doesn't remember a thing after that. Anyway, she's all right, apart from fractured clavicle, ribs and sternum, and multiple abrasions. And she just about wept for joy to hear the little girl was going to be all right. As she said, when it's someone else's child . . .'

Both nurses were silent and thoughtful for a moment. Vicky's mind inevitably went back to that other accident which had had a less happy outcome for her. But she was determined to put the past behind her now. She said levelly, 'Yes, it could have been much worse. Their guardian angel must have been on duty. How's that boy you were worried about—the motor-cyclist with the cervical fracture?'

Anna shrugged. 'Only the ventilator keeping him going.' She stirred her coffee moodily. 'Sometimes I hate the damn machines . . .'

'Mmm . . . I know what you mean,' nodded Vicky, 'but they have their uses.'

'Oh, sometimes I just feel like jacking it all in,' Anna said with an enormous sigh. 'You free tonight? How about a ride in the country and a tramp through the woods or something?'

'Yes, love to. What about transport—my bike's

out of commission at the moment.'

'Oh, forget bikes, pal,' Anna laughed. 'I run to a Metro these days.'

The girls parted company after arranging to meet that evening, and Vicky took the opportunity to telephone her cousin and enquire after Martin.

It was her aunt Celia who answered. 'Hallo, dear,' she said. 'Yes, it's me holding the fort again. Claire's taken Karen to the dentist.' Martin, she went on in answer to Vicky's enquiry, was looking better and would be going to see their GP the following day. 'Claire told us that it's the doctor who treated him at the hospital who's living in your house. Fancy that! But still, you mustn't let it make any difference to what you want to do about it. Any decisions yet?'

'We haven't got around to discussing it so far,' Vicky hedged. 'There's still some weeks of his contract to run.'

'Well, your uncle and I have been putting our heads together . . . but we'll talk about that when next we see you,' Aunt Cella said vaguely. 'When will that be, love? You're always welcome, you know.'

'I know—and thank you. At the moment, though, I'm still finiding my feet here and I'm not quite sure of my off-duty, but I'll be in touch.'

Her conscience salved, Vicky went back to get on with the afternoon's work. With discharges and admissions there was a lot of traffic on Coco Ward that afternoon. There were the technicians to take blood samples, and the anaesthetist and theatre nurses to check over and make friends with their new patients, and apprehensive parents and children to be somehow reassured and made to feel at home.

Lisa's surgery was listed for four o'clock. Her mother was with her when Vicky returned from lunch, but as yet there was no sign of Lisa's father. With Marion, her usual nurse, on days off, it fell to Vicky to take care of her.

'We've got to make you look pretty for your big moment, Lisa,' Vicky smiled, going into her room with a floral theatre gown and a flower-printed cap.

'No, I don't want to,' whimpered the nine-year-old, suddenly tearful. 'That's not pretty—it's horrible!'

Vicky held up the shapeless garment, looked at it and made a comic face. 'I agree with you, it is, isn't it? When you see Dr Simon you'll have to tell him you don't think much of his nighties.'

'I will too,' declared Lisa, but the corners of her mouth started to turn up. 'He didn't *really* choose them, did he?'

'No, not really,' Vicky laughed. 'I don't know who chooses them—the grown-up gowns are even worse, they don't have flowers on them. But it's only for a little while, then you can have your own nightie on after they've made your leg better.'

'Why hasn't Daddy come?' the little girl asked fretfully.

'I expect he got held up in the traffic, pet,' Mrs Kemp said. 'It's a long way to come from London.' She flung a despairing glance at Vicky.

'Well, I'll help Mummy to give you a nice cool wash, then we'll make your bed comfy and perhaps by that time your daddy will be here. Are you going to take Paddington with you when you go for your ride?'

Vicky talked quietly and encouragingly while she and Mrs Kemp bed-bathed Lisa, being careful not to jar her hot and painful limb. There had been no special preparation ordered for the leg—that would be done in the theatre. Finally, her toilet complete and comfort needs attended to, the theatre gown was slipped on without further argument.

Having assured herself that correct identification bracelets were in place on Lisa's wrist and ankle, Vicky checked the prescribed dose of diazepam syrup with Sister Lorne before giving it. She then left the little girl with her mother to settle down.

Lisa's father had still not appeared by the time the theatre trolley came to collect her, but, the sedative having taken effect, it scarcely mattered. Her mother and Vicky both went with her to the anaesthetic room and stayed with her until she lost consciousness.

Going back to the ward, Mrs Kemp hugged the toy bear to herself and let all her grievances come tumbling out. 'That wretched man!' she fumed. 'He's let me down in the past, time and again . . . I'm used to it. But you'd think he'd make an effort for Lisa, wouldn't you? I told him how poorly she was. And she thinks he's so wonderful . . . pop star and Santa Claus all rolled into one . . .' The woman was not far from tears.

Doing her best to be comforting, Vicky said, 'Well,

perhaps he did try, but just couldn't make it. Anyway, it'll be just as well if he sees her afterwards. It'll give her a boost, won't it?'

To give Mrs Kemp something else to think about, Vicky went on to explain the need for isolation until Lisa's wound had finished draining. 'The discharge will be infectious, so until the place has healed we shall all have to wear gowns and masks in Lisa's room and wash hands thoroughly on leaving it. Did Dr Drummond tell you that she'll probably be in plaster for a few weeks?'

Mrs Kemp nodded. They entered the ward where it was now teatime for the children. She was about to speak when she stopped short, her mouth half open, on seeing Sister Lorne coming towards them accompanied by a tall, good-looking man in a neat city suit.

He spread his hands and shrugged and gave Mrs Kemp a sweetly apologetic smile. 'It seems I've just missed Lisa. Sorry about that.'

Lisa's mother, straightfaced, said distantly: 'It's your daughter you should apologise to—it was her you disappointed. Is it too much to expect that you'll stick around and be here when she wakes up?'

'But of course I will, Ruth. That's why I came. It wasn't my fault they cancelled a train, was it?' he pleaded, his expressive dark eyes showing total innocence.

His ex-wife was only half-believing. 'It could only happen to you,' she said.

Sister Lorne looked from one to the other. 'Well, I know Lisa will be thrilled to see you, Mr Kemp, but she won't be back in the ward for some time yet. Why don't you both go to the canteen and have some tea, then you can have a chat about things, can't you?'

'OK, Sister, we'll do that. I can see you're busy in here.' Nigel Kemp turned a winning smile on Carole. 'And thanks for all you're doing for my daughter. What time shall we come back?'

'Give it a couple of hours. Shall I take Paddington, Mrs Kemp? I'll put him in Lisa's room for you.'

When the couple had gone Carole murmured: 'Wow, what a charmer!'

'Yes,' Vicky agreed, 'I should imagine he's never short of female company.'

'All right for flirting with, but not to be married to. You'd need a blind eye and a forgiving disposition with that one.'

Vicky was thoughtful. 'I bet she'd take him back, given the chance.'

'I know,' Carole sighed. 'Gluttons for punishment, some people.' She glanced at the ward clock. 'You should be off, shouldn't you?'

'Yes, but there's Lisa's room still to get ready . . .'

'Oh, I'll see to that. Off you go.'

Vicky was not sorry to escape from the confines of the hospital and other people's problems about which she could do nothing except lend a sympathetic ear and thank her lucky stars she was not in the same boat. At least if you were unattached and fancy free you had no one to please but yourselft.

Anna too was in a similar frame of mind as they

headed out in her car through the undulating Weald countryside, magnificent in its summer glory. Earlier that afternoon the fight had been lost to keep alive her motorcyclist with the spinal injury. 'I've made up my mind,' she said, negotiating a narrow, winding hill and parking in a wooded clearing at the top, 'I'm going to do midwifery. I've come to the conclusion I'd rather see people into the world than out of it.'

'Oh!' said Vicky. 'Have you decided where?'

'Yes . . . the Royal Heathside. A friend of mine trained there and it's a great place to live—Hampstead, easy to get to the West End. I could do with some action. The only trouble is, it'll be back to being a student for a time. Sickening, isn't it?'

They rambled through well-trodden paths between sweet-scented brambles and glossy-leaved beeches. Here and there the greenness was lit by swathes of rose-bay willow herb and clumps of yellow ragwort. Sitting down on the springy turf at the top of a steep grassy valley with a vista of water in the distance, Anna went on, 'How are you liking it on Kids?'

'Fine. Carole Lorne's a good manager and she really pulls her weight. The only trouble on that ward, as far as I can see, is Beryl Baxter's affair with the SHO. She's dotty about him, whereas he's prepared to take whoever's available. You know the kind.'

Anna nodded. 'Mmm—an outsized ego, some of 'em. Still, it'll be the changeover soon, won't it? Perhaps it'll fizzle out when he moves on.' Changing the subject, she said: 'Have you decided what to do about your house yet?'

'More or less—when I can get together with Simon to talk about it, that is. I thought I'd sell it to him if he really wants it: then I'll look for a flat for myself.' Vicky picked a blade of grass and chewed the sweet sappy end of it. 'I was thinking of asking if you'd like to share with me, but that's no good it you're leaving.'

'Oh, sorry, Vict,' Anna said ruefully, 'I would have liked to, but I really do think it's time I moved on.' She paused, eyeing her friend with interest. 'So you've decided on staying here, then?'

'Well, yes, for the time being. Having only just come back I need to get established somewhere, and Miss Alexander was so decent about fitting me in.'

'She would be, wouldn't she!' returned Anna with a wry smile. 'Reckon she thought it was her birthday when you showed up again. Come on, let's go and find some grub.'

Returning to the car, they drove on through the summer evening. Distant flashes of lightning heralded an approaching storm and the girls finished up back at the Black Swan just as the first large drops of rain fell.

Tonight there was no sign of Simon or Ben in the saloon bar, although there were a fair number of hospital staff about. Deciding on quiche with salad, Anna and Vicky found a corner table and settled down to enjoy their meal with a glass of wine. They had barely started when someone tapped Vicky on the shoulder. Looking up, she found Lisa's father standing there together with his ex-wife.

'Hello!' she exclaimed, glad to see that they both looked happy.

'Good evening, Nurse.' Nigel Kemp beamed from one to the other. 'I don't want to interrupt your meal, but may I buy you and your friend a drink?'

'Well, we're fine, really, thank you,' Vicky returned pleasantly. 'Did Lisa get on all right?'

Mrs Kemp nodded. 'Yes, we saw Dr Drummond and he seems well pleased with the way things went. Her leg's in a plaster, like you said.'

'I expect she was thrilled to see you when she woke up, wasn't she?' Vicky asked the personable Mr Kemp.

'I guess so—what she could see of me behind the mask,' he said with a dry smile. 'Those things scarcely make for togetherness. We didn't stay too long—she'd had an injection which made her dopey. I promised I'd look in again tomorrow, though. Well, I shall be staying on with Ruth for a few days, so that won't be difficult, will it, dear?' he went on, turning an engaging grin on his ex-wife.

Her colour deepened and she gave a selfconscious half-smile in return. 'No. Er—Nigel, don't you think we should let the girls get on with their meal?'

'Oh, *sorry*. Here's me rabbiting on, and you're supposed to be off duty,' he apologised, squeezing Vicky's shoulder. 'Now, what are you drinking? I'll order you a refill . . .'

'Another satisfied customer?' murmured Anna when the girls were once more left to themselves.

Vicky laughed. 'I hope so.' She explained the situation.

'Has he married again?' Anna asked.

'I don't know, but I'll give you one guess as to who he'll be sleeping with tonight!'

The rain was sheeting down when the girls went back to the Nurses's Home. 'At least with living in you don't have far to go in weather like this,' said Anna. 'Imagine if you were cycling from your old home! You ought to buy a car.'

'Maybe I will—when I'm in the money.' It hadn't seemed necessary when Vicky's father and Chris were alive, but now it seemed like a good idea to make herself completely independent, country buses being none too frequent.

There was still the question of her bicycle which was back at the house. Simon had said he would overhaul it, which was generous of him but asking a bit much when he must have plenty to do with his free time. On the other hand, she could scarcely make other arrangements in case he had already taken the thing to pieces. The sooner they got together and sorted out their affairs the better.

The problem was, how and when? The demands on his time were probably far greater than on hers, so it was really up to him. The best thing she could do was to ask him to name time and place and try to be accommodating.

After leaving Anna, Vicky looked in the post rack in the vestibule and collected her mail before going to her room. There were two letters—one from the

Social Secretary asking for a subscription and informing her of the social programme for the year. The other was a hand-delivered envelope written in her aunt Celia's careful handwriting. Opening this, Vicky found an airgraph from Tim, a male nurse friend in Australia, together with a scribbled note from her aunt which read:

> 'Dear Vicky, I forgot to mention this had arrived for you. I also thought I ought to tell you straightaway what your uncle and I had been discussing, just in case you get to talking business with Dr Drummond before we see you again. The fact is, we thought we might like to buy your house for Claire and Geoff. They've really outgrown that little place of theirs. We haven't said anything about it to them yet—if you can keep things ticking over until Geoff gets back from abroad it would help. It would be nice to keep it in the family, don't you think? And I'm sure it would just suit them—that's if you haven't decided to keep it for yourself. Anyway, think about it. See you soon, Lots of love, Celia.'

'Oh, no!' Vicky groaned. Just when she had finally got it all sorted out in her mind, well-meaning Celia had to go and complicate matters! Now she had a whole new problem.

CHAPTER FIVE

CLOSING her bedroom window against the rain, Vicky stood for a moment watching its relentless drive caught in the beam of street lamps and car headlights. It was cleansing and refreshing, washing away the dust of summer. She wished her own problem could be as easily washed away.

Before reading her aunt's note Vicky had been feeling quite liberated after deciding to be practical and let Simon buy the house. Now, with Aunt Celia putting her spoke in, she was once more at a loss. One thing was for sure; she was going to have to disappoint somebody. Vicky sighed heavily and half-wished she had never come back from Australia. Then she would never have met Simon Drummond, which would have made things a whole lot easier.

After some reflection she came to the conclusion that there was only one thing to do, in order to keep things 'ticking over' as her aunt had suggested. Stay out of Simon's way, if she could, for as long as possible.

Idly Vicky slit open the airgraph from Tim and flopped on the bed to read it. That at least contained cheering news. He had decided to blow his savings on a trip to England—'before I get sucked into the matrimonial whirlpool,' he wrote. 'Of course, it could also be that I'm missing a certain little Pommie who walked out on us . . .'

Smiling to herself, Vicky read on. She knew Tim well enough not to take those kind of remarks too seriously. He was by nature gregarious and full of fun and had been a good friend to her ever since her arrival at the hospital in Sydney. Living in the same block of staff units, he had more or less taken her under his wing. It had helped, too, that his family had connections in Kent, and Tim's parents had welcomed her into their home, glad to talk about the old country.

Tim's letter said that he would be arriving at the end of July, after which he'd get in touch with her. Feeling considerably heartened at the prospect, Vicky went to bed looking forward to seeing him and planning all the things they could do together. With the Australian nation only just celebrating its bicentenary, they had no heritage to compare with places like Canterbury Cathedral, or the Tower of London, or even Hever Castle, or Knole, or any of the great houses of Kent. She would enjoy showing him around.

On duty at one o'clock the following day, Vicky found the usually easy-going Sister Lorne looking thoroughly indignant as she put down the telephone. 'I don't believe it!' she complained, running a hand through her short brown curls. 'That was Miss Alexander, Vicky. She wants you back in A and E.'

Vicky frowned. 'When?'

'Straight away.' Carole shuffled some case notes together impatiently. 'Apparently Bonner asked for you. One of her team's gone sick, and as we're not fully stretched here at the moment, I could hardly quibble.' She spread her hands in despair. 'Things could change any minute, couldn't they? I don't know! She sends me a decent children's nurse and then whisks you away again.'

'Oh dear, sorry about that,' said Vicky. 'I was warned I'd be moved around to begin with. Is it only for today?'

'I hope so, or I shall say my piece at the next staff meeting.' Carole gave an exaggerated sigh. 'You like it here, don't you?'

'Oh yes, of course I do. Miss Alexander said she'd try to fit me in here permanently, but I suppose she's got a difficult job, keeping everywhere properly staffed during the holiday season.'

'Huh,' scoffed Carole, 'you can't be the only nurse she can juggle with. It's Bonner throwing her weight about, I expect. You'd better go, then.'

Although Vicky preferred the happy disorder of the children's ward to the stark drama of A and E, this time she was not altogether sorry to have been transferred. It would at least solve her immediate problem of keeping out of Simon Drummond's way—or so she fondly imagined.

Sister Bonner welcomed her warmly. 'One of my staff nurses has gone off with a bad back, and there was no one I could think of better to take her place. You didn't mind, did you, dear? Half the students are frightened to death coming to A and E. And you're so good in a crisis—you're wasted anywhere else.'

Vicky laughed. 'Thanks for the compliment, but there can be crises on the wards as well.'

'Yes, I know,' agreed Sister Bonner, 'but not to the same extent, and you can't blame me for fighting for my own department, can you? Cubicle six, please, Vicky. There's a thirteen-year-old lad in there—a playground stabbing in abdo, possible perforation of the small bowel.' She picked up the ringing telephone and held her hand over the mouthpiece for a moment. 'The third-year with him is new to Casualty—make sure she knows what she's doing. His mum's in the waiting area if you need any more information.'

By the time Vicky finished work at nine-thirty that night she had seen rather more of Simon Drummond than she would have done had she stayed on Coco Ward, since three out of the many patients she dealt with were children requiring his attention. Not that there was time for any talk between them other than that called for in the course of their work.

Even so, the matter of their unfinished business spoiled, for Vicky, what would otherwise have been an absorbing working relationship. Outwardly she remained her calm, capable self. Inwardly, her stomach lurched whenever the registrar's keen blue eyes met hers. Nothing was mentioned about their private affairs, yet the subject was ever present and explosive, at least, in Vicky's mind. And as if that were not enough, she felt again that subtle alchemy which seemed to accompany all her dealings with this man.

But she had survived, Vicky reminded her self with a sense of relief at the end of the day. So long as she concentrated on the work, all would be plain sailing. It was stupid to get in a state over things in advance. Plenty of time for that when the crunch came, if it ever did.

Being assigned to Casualty for the whole of the next week, Vicky was pleased to find herself coping well with the emotive demands of the job. Her last Friday on duty, however, brought a domestic accident which called for all her reserves of level-headedness and compassion.

Six-year-old Hannah had been playing with matches and set fire to her clothing. A helpful neighbour coming to the rescue had swathed her in a wet tablecloth and rushed her to the hospital along with her distraught mother. The child was too shocked to do more than whimper piteously, but the mother was bordering on hysteria.

Firmly but kindly Sister Bonner put an arm around the woman and led her away to take details, allowing Moira Smith, the Casualty Officer, to concentrate on the patient without hindrance.

Vicky, assisting, spoke soothingly to the little girl while carefully lifting back the damp cloth to expose the injury. Involuntarily she shuddered at the sight of the small burned body, bits of charred clothing still adhering to the wound.

'My God!' the doctor breathed, raising shocked eyes to her helper. She seemed almost stunned to inaction by the extent of the damage. 'Wh-what the hell can we do?' she muttered.

'Better get an IV going, hadn't we?' Vicky spoke in a low, urgent voice, her own immediate checks having found the child's pulse feeble and her blood pressure falling.

'Yes—er—right. Y-you get things ready. I'll see if I can get hold of Simon.' Moira, her face chalk-white, put a hand to her mouth as she hurried from the cubicle.

Moira Smith was normally a competent doctor, but this particular casualty had visibly shaken her. She had probably gone to throw up, Vicky surmised. She herself felt sickened at the severity of the burns, but she drew a steadying breath and carried on with what needed to be done. Speed was of the essence, or the child might not survive.

'Hannah, my pet, I'll try not to hurt you, I'm just going to put a clean cloth over the bad place,' Vicky said, opening out a sterile towel and laying it gently over the burn. 'When the doctor comes he'll give you something to take the pain away. Your mummy's still here—you can see her in a minute . . .' She continued talking in a quiet, comforting voice while she got together the infusion equipment and other things which would be needed.

To her enormous relief when Moira reappeared she was accompanied by Simon, who lost no time in starting restorative measures.

'This'll need cleaning up under a GA,' he declared, 'but the first priority is to get some fluid into her. Come on!' he prompted the wan-faced Moira. 'Let's get this drip going—fast! And you, Nurse,' he barked over his shoulder while scrubbing his hands at the basin, 'hurry up with that morphine. Stat means *now*!'

Although as distressed as they all were at the child's plight, Vicky responded with alacrity to Simon's brusque demands. She knew that his impatience sprang from his desire to ease pain and replace vital lost body fluids as quickly as possible.

When all was done that could be done for the time being, arrangements were then made for Hannah's transfer to the Special Burns Unit at East Grinstead.

Explaining the situation to her distressed mother, Simon consoled: 'She'll be in good hands there, Mrs Brand. We haven't attempted to treat the burn—that's best left until she's over the shock. Later she's going to need skin grafts, and East Grinstead are experts in that field. Luckily her face escaped damage; at least that's something to be thankful for, isn't it?' he added kindly.

It was Vicky's lot to go with the child in the ambulance to monitor the drip and be generally supportive. As they sped along with the siren wailing, the mother stroked the hand of her now sedated small daughter and glanced at Vicky, tragic-eyed. 'She will be all right, won't she, Nurse?'

'She's every chance,' Vicky returned encouragingly. 'They have the best facilities at the Burns Unit. I expect she'll be nursed exposed there. That might seem a bit strange at first, but it does away with a lot of painful dressings.' She paused before saying, 'Healing is going to take time, though,

Mrs Brand. You must be prepared for a fairly long job.'

The mother nodded. 'Kids!' she sighed. 'Bang goes our summer holiday.'

'How did she come to get hold of the matches?'

'Oh, she's such a naughty little thing—she must have taken them out of my bag. I keep them there with my ciggies. I swear to God I'll never have another box in the house. Better give up smoking, I suppose. Her dad's always on at me about it.'

Vicky said nothing. At the back of her mind was a memory of how she'd rescued a box of matches from her cousin Claire's youngest boy. She wished Claire could have seen this maimed child.

It was after seven before the ambulance dropped Vicky back at Wealdwood Hospital where, collecting her belongings from the staff room in A and E, she prepared to go belatedly off duty.

'Well, dear, did she make the journey all right?' Sister Bonner asked.,

'Yes, we got her there with no hangups.' Vicky gave a heartfelt sigh. 'That's the least of her problems, isn't it?'

'It is indeed,' the Sister agreed. 'By the way . . .' she took a buff envelope from the drawer and, with a curious smile, gave it to Vicky, 'Dr Drummond left this for you. I gather he approved of the way you handled yourself. I told him you were always one of the best girls.'

Vicky studied the *Miss Victoria Chalfont* scrawled on the envelope, and grinned. 'What's this then, an apology for snapping my head off?'

'Huh! That'd make history,' declared Sister Bonner. 'Doctors don't go in for apologies as a rule. Still, they're not all tarred with the same brush, I suppose.'

Feeling slightly embarrassed, Vicky stuffed the letter into her pocket to read in the privacy of her own room. She imagined it must be something to do with the house and she didn't feel like going into all that with Sister Bonner at the time.

Back at the Nurses' Home Maddy, the girl in the next room, met her on the stairs and invited her in for coffee and a chat, so that it was some time before she was able to open the registrar's note. When she did, the message simply read: 'I shall be grateful if you will ring me at home tonight, after nine, if you possibly can. Please try! Yours, Simon.'

Vicky's stomach flipped. There was no cause to feel nervous, yet she did. It was the first time she had worked with Simon in a life-or-death heartrending situation. At the time he was the one who had been uptight. Her own other self had taken over; the steady, reassuring side of her that didn't panic and could somehow find the right thing to say and do in an emergency. So if it had nothing to do with her handling of the burns case, it must be personal. No point in speculating. She would find out soon enough.

It was ten o'clock before she eventually plucked up courage to make the call, after having some supper and washing her hair.

'Ah, Vicky,' Simon greeted her. 'Are you all right?'

'Fine!' There was a short pause, while he seemed to be waiting for her to elaborate. She laughed. 'Was that why you asked me to ring . . . to enquire after my health?'

'Yes and no. I was a bit concerned about you. I know you were not too keen to be back in Casualty, but you did well this afternoon. You were almost too controlled.'

There was another small silence before she answered. 'Oh! Well, I'm not in floods of tears or anything, if that's what you were thinking. I'm quite good at coping with other people's problems. My own are entirely different.'

'Yes, of course. And that's the only way to deal with the traumas we meet, isn't it, to distance oneself.'

Vicky laughed again. 'And here was I wondering if you wanted to apologise for jumping down my throat in the heat of the moment!'

'Did I do that?' He sounded surprised. 'Well, don't take it to heart. I was scared we were going to lose the kid. But we didn't, did we?'

'No. And the responsibility did rest with you, so I'm prepared to be magnanimous.'

He let that pass. 'What I really wanted to talk about is your bicycle—I've managed to fix it.'

'My bike! Oh, thanks, Simon,' she said, pleased. 'Did you need to spend money on it? What do I owe you?'

'Oh! Nothing to speak of. Sister Bonner tells me you're off for the weekend and that then you're on nights, so I thought it might be convenient for you to come and collect it before then.'

'Yes. Er . . . could I come tomorrow?'

'OK. I'll be at the hospital in the morning. I could pick you up at the Nurses' Home after lunch. Say three o'clock, would that suit you?'

'Great!' she said. And the glow of pleasure she felt had less to do with having her bicycle restored then the prospect of seeing Simon without the pressures of work. Even though it might not be possible to avoid talking about the house.

The following afternoon, the weather being overcast, Vicky dressed in black cotton trousers and a roomy bright pink sweater, having in mind her cycle ride home. The forecast was for more rain, so she stuffed her waterproof kagoule into her shoulder bag for good measure. With heart beating at considerably more than the norm, she skipped down to the front entrance and waited, looking for the red BMW among the moving traffic.

It rolled up smoothly in a few moments and Simon pushed the car door open for her. She settled in beside him, smiling up into his strong, handsome face. 'Thank you, Simon. It's awfully nice of you to have gone to all this bother on my account. I'll be quite glad to have my trusty old wheels back again.'

'My pleasure.' Backing the car, he turned it and eased his way through the congested grounds until they reached the main road. 'Vicky, before we go back to the house, I'd like to make a call. That is, if you're not pushed for time.'

'No,' she said, 'I've nothing special planned. I thought of going to my aunt's later on, but they're not expecting me.'

'Good!' He gave her the sideways teasing grin that was inclined to make her limbs feel weak, 'So you can come and see my aunt instead.'

'Is that the one you told me about—the one you used to spend holidays with?'

Simon nodded. 'I found a book I thought she'd like—in an antique shop—she collects old books, amongst other things.' He gestured towards the map pocket. 'It's in there, have a look.'

In the compartment Vicky found a paper bag containing a slim volume. It was bound in brown leather and tooled in gold, its title *The Rubáiyát of Omar Khayyám*. 'Oh, lovely!' she exclaimed, glancing through, her eyes lighting on many well-remembered and poignant lines. She quoted in a dreamy voice: '*There was a door to which I found no key: There was a veil past which I could not see.* Funny how a poet can sum up in a few words exactly how it is sometimes.'

'I'm not into poetry myself,' Simon admitted, 'but I like this one's philosophy. Time flies . . . and we should make the most of what we have while we have it.'

Vicky closed the book thoughtfully. 'Is it your aunt's birthday or something?'

'No, but she's a lovely lady. Her husband died a few years ago and her own son's in the USA. I feel sort of responsible—I don't go and see her as often as I should. This gives me an excuse to pop in. Besides, I'm sure she'll be interested to meet my landlady,' he added, giving her a mischievous grin.

Vicky frowned, eyeing his square-jawed profile and the shapely lips puckering with humour. 'She doesn't know you're coming? You're sure she won't mind you bringing me? I mean, she won't have had time to comb her hair or dust the mantelpiece or anything. My aunt Celia would be most put out.'

Simon threw back his head and roared with laughter. 'Prepare yourself for a culture shock, Vicky. My aunt Vinny wouldn't turn a hair even if Charles and Diana showed up!'

They had passed the Pantiles now and were crossing the Common towards Fordcombe. Simon turned in through the immense wrought-iron gates to a private estate where large mansions sat well back from the gravelled road, fronted by vistas of green parkland. Some of the houses were well kept up, others a little dilapidated. A gardener sat on a motor-mower, whirring his way around the lawns, and Simon gave him a wave as they passed.

'Here we are,' he said. The car crunched down a gravelled drive and came to rest where it ended, in front of a once grand manor house with gnarled wistaria curling its way along the still elegant terrace railings. He took the book from where it still lay on Vicky's lap. 'Mind how you go up the steps, they're rather worn.'

With some misgivings Vicky followed the registrar, who bounded up the wide, flagged steps to where the outer heavy door stood open. It gave on to a glassed-in area bursting with potted plants of every description. He pulled the bell-cord before bowling through into the lofty, panelled entrance hall, where he bellowed, 'Vinny . . . where are you?'

A door opened in the panelling and a large lady appeared, her fleshy face wreathing in smiles at the sight of him.

'Simon darling! How lovely to see you! I must have known—I just popped some scones in the oven. The only time I can get into my kitchen is when Sarah goes home for the weekend.' She wiped floury hands on the tea-towel she held, draped it over the carved oak banister rail, and came flowing towards him, arms outstretched.

Vicky watched with a smile, realising that it would take more than unexpected visitors to worry this matriarch. The hem of her Liberty-print skirt was coming down, there was a button undone on her moss-green shirt-blouse, and the heavy braid of iron-grey hair was escaping its confining pins. But, as Simon had said, she was totally unconcerned about receiving visitors.

Now, after embracing her nephew, she beamed at Vicky and said, in her deep fruity voice, 'And who's this you've brought to see me, darling? She's very pretty.'

He made the introductions, explaining briefly who Vicky was, and the two women cordially shook hands.

'Present for you,' Simon said, handing his aunt the book.

'For me?' she exclaimed with delight, taking the volume from its wrapping. 'Dear boy! I hope you didn't pay a fortune for this . . . it's exquisite!'

Mills & Boon
BEST SELLER ROMANCE
The Silken Trap
CHARLOTTE LAMB
Mills & Boon
BEST SELLER ROMANCE
Green Mountain Man
Mills & Boon
Mills & Boon

'No. I dazzled the sales girl with my charm.'

'That I can believe!' she smiled, and kissed him again. 'Thank you so much. Well, you must excuse me while I go and rescue my scones. Why don't you take Victoria into the garden and show her my blue Himalayan poppies? They're at their best at the moment.'

'OK, but don't hang about. It's you we've come to see, not your poppies,' he returned with a tolerant grin.

'I'll be with you in two shakes of a lamb's tail,' she promised, and disappeared back into the kitchen.

Simon ushered Vicky out into the woodland garden and along the border of rare and lovely plants which his aunt had nurtured. 'She's quite a girl, itsn't she?' he said.

'She is that,' Vicky agreed with a soft laugh. 'Oh, aren't these a heavenly colour!' She bent her nose to the golden anthers of the brilliant sky-blue poppies which grew in drifts between the shrubs. 'Not much perfume, but you can't have everything.'

He stooped to break off a rock-pink growing between the large stones that bordered the path. 'There you are, if you want perfume,' he said, holding the flower to her nose.

His eyes, smiling into hers, were a deeper blue than the poppies and even more breathtaking. Vicky felt a sudden longing for time to stand still, a confusion of desires as wild as the garden that surrounded them. Her breath came quickly and she swallowed when Simon cupped her cheek while tucking the flower into her hair.

She was left wondering what might have happened had not Aunt Vinny joined them at that moment, bringing normality with her. 'Oh, that flower just matches your jumper, my dear,' she approved. 'Well, what do you think of my blue beauties?'

All in all it was a fascinating afternoon. After wandering further into the garden to find the brook where Simon had played as a child, Vicky was introduced to the pet white duck which slept in the kennel with the shaggy dog of doubtful pedigree. Then there was tea and scones in the high-ceilinged sitting-room with its worn silk-covered furniture and threadbare carpet and old oil paintings hanging askew in battered gilt frames. Later, a tour of the mansion revealed countless precious objects, including the collection of ancient books which was Lavinia's delight, and the special room with its battalions of model soldiers which had belonged to her husband.

'I keep them here in memory of Guy,' Lavinia said with no trace of sadness. 'My son's not interested in them, and neither are my nephews. That nice Dr Milden who treated my nose said he'd like to see them, but he hasn't called. You must bring him, Simon.'

'I'll see what I can arrange,' he promised.

'And do let me *know*, darling,' she boomed, 'so that I can look presentable. I might be up to my elbows in mud instead of making scones. Heaven knows what your young friend must think of me!'

Vicky laughed. 'I've thoroughly enjoyed myself.

It's nice to be completely informal sometimes.'

'Ah yes, there's all that precision and protocol in hospitals, isn't there? It can't be easy, but we couldn't do without you. Do come and see me whenever you like, my dear. I keep open house here.'

The ornate long-case clock in the hall was chiming six as they left the house, Vicky with a potted begonia which Simon's aunt insisted on giving her, along with careful instructions about not overwatering.

'That took a bit longer than I expected,' Simon remarked cheerfully when they had been waved on their way, 'but you weren't doing anything special, were you?'

'No,' she returned, 'and I really enjoyed meeting your aunt and seeing all her goodies. But I wouldn't care to live in a place like that, fascinating though it is. It must cost a bomb to keep warm in winter.'

'It does, but that doesn't seem to bother her, and she likes the space. The local drama society meets there, and the historical society, and I don't know who else. She's got lots of friends. It's fine, providing she keeps well.' Simon smiled at Vicky. 'The ancestral hall is all right for some, but personally I prefer a house with mod cons. That's why I'm glad you came with me this afternoon. I wanted you to see why I'm hooked on your home. It's the first really welcoming place I've ever lived in. My own parents have just taken it into their heads to buy a barn of a place in the wilds of Scotland. It's about as inviting as Colditz!'

Vicky's blithe and buoyant mood suddenly took

a nose-dive. That intimate moment in the wild garden had gone to her head like potent wine, making her wonder if Simon were attracted to her. After all, he had gone to the trouble of mending her bicycle, and taken her to see his aunt, and been altogether charming. Now she discovered that he was merely being agreeable because he wanted to buy her house!

Smiling a trifle wryly at her own naïvety, she took the pink from her hair and studied its bunched, scented petals. 'And there was I thinking it might have been for the pleasure of my company!' she returned in a teasing voice.

'Is that what you would have preferred me to say?' he asked, sounding amused.

'No, not if it wasn't true.'

He slowed the car while a brilliant cock pheasant sauntered from one side of the country lane to the other. Then, picking up speed again, he replied: 'It depends on what you mean by true. Truth isn't always palatable. But this time I can genuinely say, with my hand on my heart,' he added with mock-solemnity, 'that of course I've enjoyed your company. The obvious doesn't need to be spelt out. Does it, Vicky?'

She wished she hadn't started this conversation. 'Oh, for goodness' sake, it was only a joke. No need to hold a flipping inquest!'

Simon laughed at that. 'I'm glad your sense of humour's in good working order. But I wasn't joking. I have enjoyed being with you.'

'Good, that's established. I'm *so* glad.' Vicky

laid her flower carefully on the dashboard.

He gave her a fleeting sideways glance, his lips restraining a smile. 'Shall we carry on playing the truth game?'

'It depends upon what you mean by true,' she repeated mischievously.

'I mean, about whether you've come to any decision yet, about selling me the house?'

Ah! So that *was* the subject uppermost in his mind. Vicky sighed and scratched her head. She really couldn't blame him. After all, it must be unsettling for him, not knowing what she intended. 'Simon, I honestly thought I had,' she said, 'and then *my* aunt came up with another idea. Now I don't know what to do . . .'

'Complications?' Simon darted her a swift sideways glance. 'Can't say I'm surprised,' he went on. 'If you haven't actually been going out of your way to avoid me—and I'm not at all sure about that—you certainly haven't tried to seek me out.' He shot her another equivocal look.

She kept her eyes on the passing scene, not knowing what to say. She hadn't thought it obvious, her efforts to avoid him except when work demanded it. He had evidently been much more aware than she realised.

'Oh well,' Simon picked out a cassette and slipped it into place, 'if there are weighty matters to be discussed perhaps we should leave it until we get back to the house.'

They passed the rest of the journey making fairly innocuous conversation to undemanding background music. It didn't help at all as far as Vicky was concerned. His forbearance had managed to make her feel guilty, which in turn made her cross, because it all seemed to be going wrong, and it was not her fault.

CHAPTER SIX

BACK at the house Simon discarded his jacket and tie, leaving them draped casually over the banister-post at the bottom of the stairs. 'Coffee?' he asked.

'Please.' Vicky nodded and followed him through into the kitchen, watching as he got busy filling the kettle and spooning coffee grounds into the jug.

It was only the second time she had been in the house since her return, but she felt immediately at home there and it seemed odd to be entertained by the doctor in these familiar surroundings. To give herself something to do she got the mugs out of the crockery cupboard, and the milk from the fridge, and found the sugar, remembering his sweet tooth. It also delayed for a little while having to talk about the subject on both their minds.

Soon, however, the coffee was ready, and she sat opposite him at the scrubbed pine table, and there was no avoiding his frank, questioning gaze.

Vicky smiled slightly, lowered her lashes and resorted to adding more milk to her drink.

'Come on, get it off your chest,' Simon encouraged briskly. 'You're not going to sell to me. You want me to leave, is that it?'

'No, no, it's not like that at all.' She raised troubled amber-brown eyes to his. 'I was quite prepared for you to have it, until the other day. My aunt suddenly came up with the idea that they'd like the house for my cousin. That's Martin's mother, if you remember? They're pushed for space where they are and my aunt thinks this would be ideal for them. They've been awfully good to me, all of them, so . . .' Vicky shrugged helplessly, 'I don't really see how I can refuse, apart from if I said I wanted to live here again myself.'

'Oh, I see,' Simon scratched his lean cheek thoughtfully, 'and I suppose you'd really prefer your cousin to have it?'

She sighed heavily. 'I'm honestly not bothered. There's no point in being sentimental about it. I mean, it's only a house, isn't it? On the other hand, you're settled in and you like it here . . .' Vicky sighed again. 'I-I'm terribly sorry, Simon, I really am, but I can't see any way out.'

There was a brooding silence while they both drank coffee. Then, in apparent acceptance, the doctor said levelly: 'Right, so I'll have to look for something else, won't I?'

'Oh, must you be so damned reasonable?' Vicky wailed. 'You make me feel awful. Why don't you blow your top, get mad at me, or something?'

He curbed a smile. 'On the whole I'm a most reasonable man, you'll find. But that *or something* tempts me. What would you like me to do—wallop you, or woo you?'

She tossed her head impatiently. 'Don't be ridiculous! I don't want to ask you to go, but unless you've got any bright ideas . . .'

'We-ell,' he drawled, eyeing her tentatively, 'there is an instant solution which comes to mind. How about you moving in here with me?'

Although Carole Lorne had playfully suggested it, coming from Simon, it took Vicky's breath away. Her cheeks flushed and for a moment her mouth gaped. She swallowed and drew a deep breath before answering: 'Are you serious?'

'Never more so. Unless, of course, it doesn't appeal to you.'

She chewed her thumbnail, her head in a whirl. 'I don't know. Would it work?'

'Why not?' he challenged. 'You could cover yourself by extending my lease for, say, three months to see how it goes. The place is big enough for the two of us, surely, without getting in each other's way. And, if you were living here and not actually selling, then your relatives could hardly take offence, could they? Meanwhile,' Simon went on, a roguish gleam in his eyes, 'they might even get around to finding something else to buy.'

Vicky smiled. 'You may or may not be reasonable, Dr Drummond, but you're certainly devious!'

'I prefer to call it diplomacy. Well, shall we give it a go?'

Excitement stirred inside her. The prospect was certainly attractive, but she wasn't sure whether it would be wise. Simon was a masterful character who already made a strong appeal to her physical senses. He obviously saw this partnership as one of convenience and, but for the fact that he had rented her house, she would probably still only be on polite nodding terms with him at the hospital. So where was the problem? Even if they lived together under the same roof they wouldn't see all that much of each other, what with her working hours and his. She was sensible enough not to lose her head, wasn't she?

Searching for possible obstacles, she recalled the clutter in the spare room and asked: 'What about your brother—what will he say?'

'Paul? It's nothing to do with him—he only drops in when it suits him. I'll get him to clear his stuff out of that room if that's the one you'd like.'

'No, that's all right,' she said, 'I'd be quite happy to have my old room.'

'That's the pink-and-white one, next to mine?' Simon nodded. 'Yes, I can see you in there.'

Vicky was tempted to ask him who had used it recently, remembering the subtle trace of fragrance when she had looked in, but she thought better of it. It was none of her business who he entertained.

'If I come,' she went on, 'we'd lead our own separate lives, wouldn't we? I mean, I wouldn't expect to be part of the deal, to look after all the domestic arrangements or whatever.'

Simon gave an expansive gesture. 'My dear girl, you'd be free as a bird. Mrs Marks does my chores and her husband the garden, and that's the way it can stay. You can please yourself what you do. Living here for a time would help you to make a permanent decision one way or the other, wouldn't it?' he added persuasively. 'Speaking personally, I should find it very pleasant to have someone about to share my thoughts with now and again.'

Still looking for snags, she queried, 'What about our social lives? Naturally I should want to have my friends here as and whenever. That wouldn't worry you?'

'Of course not, providing you don't object to mine. No strings either way.'

'Well, in that case,' Vicky replied thoughtfully, 'perhaps we could give it a go. I-I could hang on to my hospital room for a bit, just in case it doesn't work out.'

He laughed. 'What are you scared of? Me, or yourself, or those ghosts from the past?'

She wrinkled her nose at him. 'Put it down to my natural caution.'

Simon looked inordinately pleased with life. 'Right! That's settled, then. Terrific. Well, I don't know about you, Vicky, but I'm hungry.' He got to his feet and strode to the refrigerator. 'What do you fancy? There's some cold chicken, or I could do you egg and bacon, or there's moussaka in the freezer which won't take long to microwave.'

She chose the cold chicken as being the least trouble. They ate it with chutney and crusty rolls, and Simon opened a bottle of hock to celebrate their partnership.

Night had come on and with it some squally rain by the time they had finished talking about the events of the day and future arrangements. Checking the time, Vicky saw with some surprise that it was after eleven. 'And I haven't even looked at my bicycle yet,' she reminded him. 'Have I got lights?'

'Batteries!' Simon snapped his fingers. 'I knew there was something I meant to get. Well, you can't ride back without lights, and anyway, it's a rotten night. You'd better stay—try out your old room for size.'

Since he was apparently not offering to drive her back to the Nurses's Home, she had no choice but to agree as the last bus would have gone.

'I probably won't see you in the morning,' Simon told her, washing their supper dishes in a businesslike fashion. 'I'll be away before eight—I've got a meeting in Canterbury. You'll find your bike in the garage. And you've got keys to the house, I presume? Move in whenever you like. I may not be back until late on Monday.'

'Well, I'll probably leave moving in until I've finished my nights.' Vicky picked up a tea-towel and began drying. 'It'll be more convenient then. Tomorrow I shall have to go and break the news to Aunt Celia,' she said, privately not relishing the prospect.

'Oh dear, is that going to be difficult?' Wiping his hands, Simon turned to watch her as she put the cutlery away, and she suddenly found herself the focus of his concentrated gaze.

Her blood began pulsating wildly. She wondered yet again whether she was mad to have agreed to this arrangement. 'She's bound to be disappointed, and probably disapproving,' she said, forcing herself to speak lightly, 'but there you are, you can't please everyone.' She hung up the hand-towel which he had left in a bundle on the worktop. 'I'll say goodnight, then, Simon. Thanks for everything,' she added with a shy smile.

'No, thank *you*, Vicky.' As if it were the most natural thing in the world, he rested his hands on her shoulders and murmured: 'Thanks for being so accommodating,' and planted a kiss on her upturned face. 'Goodnight, sleep well,' he said, smiling down into her wide luminous eyes.

For a moment she stood spellbound, breath suspended. Her heart pounded in her ears as her body reacted wantonly to his touch. It made her want to experience more—the warm, hard strength of his arms about her, not keeping distance between them like this.

It was only seconds before he released her, slipped his thumbs into his trouser pockets and carried on talking. 'Mrs Marks keeps the beds made in case of visitors. And you'll know where to find towels and things. Off you go, then.'

'Yes, right.' Taking a grip on herself, Vicky turned and went upstairs to the bathroom. She splashed her flushed cheeks with cold water, as if the action could clear her head of the doubts and uncertainties that crowded in. Patting her face dry, she regarded her own stupefied image in the mirror and gave herself a stern reminder of the facts. She was here because it suited *him*, and for no other reason, and she had better not forget it.

Back in her own bedroom, drawing the oyster-pink curtains as she had done so often in those days before disaster struck, it was difficult to believe that she was really there. Her bookcase still housed the collection of books she had gathered over the years, and she picked out a favourite bedside book to occupy her mind as she slipped naked beneath the duvet. But with her thoughts spinning round in her head like a dog chasing its tail, it was impossible to concentrate. Presently she gave up the struggle and put out the light.

It must have been midnight before she heard Simon ascending the stairs and closing the door of his own room; the room which had been her parents'. She lay listening to the small sounds of his presence; the clink of keys, a drawer opened and shut, running water in the en-suite bathroom, the click of a light switch.

She remembered the warm pressure of his lips and the tempting male scent of his skin when he had kissed her goodnight. Just a friendly kiss, nothing more, she again reminded herself. Yet her pulse still quickened at the memory of it. 'What the hell am I getting into?' she pondered uneasily. It struck her that keeping her head might not be quite so easy as she had at first imagined.

Waking the following morning, it took Vicky a little while to remember where she was. Through half-closed eyes, she absorbed the strong thrust of sunlight through the delicate weave of the curtains as her mind replayed the events of the past twenty-four hours.

Surprisingly, after a slow start she had slept well. Stirring herself sufficiently to check her wristwatch on the bedside cabinet, she was surprised to find it was after nine a.m. Outside, the peace of the morning was disturbed only by the distant whirr of a lawnmower and the muted cooing of a wood-pigeon. In the house itself there was no sound. Vicky supposed that Simon must already have left for Canterbury. He must have been very quiet, unless it was his leaving which had awoken her.

Stretching lazily, she reflected on the oddities of life. Who would have thought that coming back to England with ideas of selling the house she would instead find herself moving in with the tenant? And he one of the senior hospital doctors at that! What Aunt Celia would think was another matter, but Vicky pushed that to the back of her mind for the time being. She only knew that for some incomprehensible reason she felt absurdly, blissfully, dangerously exhilarated. As though she were poised on the brink of some momentous adventure.

Gazing around the well-remembered room, she revelled in the thought of having her old home all to herself again, at least for today. Oh, it was good to be back, despite past sad associations and present hazards. When she had showered and had some breakfast she would go on a leisurely tour of remembrance before searching out her bicycle. Later, of course, there would be Aunt Celia to mollify, but Vicky hoped she would understand. And if she didn't, too bad.

Springing out of bed, she inched open her bedroom door and called cautiously, 'Simon?' With no reply forthcoming she made cheerfully for the bathroom and enjoyed an invigorating shower. Once more dressed in yesterday's black cotton trousers and pink sweater, she drew a comb hastily through her damp brown locks and skipped downstairs to the kitchen.

There on the table, anchored under a pot of Marmite, was a scrawled note from Simon. 'Vicky', it read, 'hope you slept well. I forgot to say Mrs Marks comes in tomorrow to clean. If you need help with moving your stuff I shall be glad to oblige. Yours, Simon.'

On Monday Vicky was due to report for her week of night duty. She had definitely decided not to move in until afterwards. Therefore, unless Simon was called in for an emergency, it could be some time before she was likely to see him again. Which made the prospect of night duty seem even more unwelcome. But then she had always loathed nights. Either you were boringly slack and had to fight a battle to stay alert in the small hours, or there would be one crisis after another and not enough hands to cope. Never the happy medium.

Switching on the radio for company, Vicky hummed along with the cheerful Sunday morning music while she made toast and coffee. With her thoughts straying in a dozen directions as she sat down to her solitary meal, she failed to hear the front door being opened, and she almost shot out of her chair when a tall, jeans-clad stranger appeared in the kitchen doorway.

'Hi!' the intruder exclaimed, looking equally taken aback to find her there. 'Sorry if I startled you.' He grinned broadly and pushed a hand through the unruly dark hair crowning his cheerful, outdoors face. 'Didn't expect to find a lady here. My brother's obviously been keeping quiet about you.'

Her alarm gave way to relief. 'Oh,' she smiled back, 'I suppose you must be Paul?'

'Yep, that's me. Who are you?'

'Vicky—Vicky Chalfont. I own the house.'

Paul's dark eyebrows lifted, then he laughed. 'Get away!' Coming further into the kitchen, he arranged his long legs saddlewise around the back of a chair, rested his chin on his hands and studied her with interest. 'It didn't dawn on us that you were—well, scarcely out of nappies.'

'Do you mind!' laughed Vicky.

'No, not at all. And Simon didn't tell me you'd turned up. Where is he, anyway? Is he here?'

'No, he left earlier this morning to go to Canterbury.'

'I see.' Paul scratched his rugged cheek and frowned. 'Well, no, I don't really. I haven't spoken to Sime lately. So what's going on? Are you back for good, or are you just checking up on your property?'

Vicky couldn't help liking this forthright young man who, she guessed, might be somewhere about her own age. 'Yes, I imagine you must be a bit puzzled. Actually I came to pick up my bicycle last night. Your brother was good enough to fix it for me, but the lights weren't working, so he invited me to stay the night and go back to the Nurses' Home this morning.' She half rose. 'Can I get you some coffee?'

'It's all right, I'll get it.' He motioned to her to stay seated and looked more mystified than ever. 'Did I hear you say—*Nurses' Home*?'

Vicky nodded and smiled. 'Yes, I'm a nurse. I used to work at Wealdwood Hospital before I went abroad, and now I've come back there. It was a shock to both of us, Simon and me discovering we were working at the same place.'

'I bet! Extraordinary thing!' Paul shook his head and set about making himself a drink while she brought him up to date with the situation.

'Your brother seemed to feel guilty about me having to live at the Nurses' Home, although there's no reason why he should. Anyway, he suggested we might as well share for a time to see how it goes. I haven't moved in yet, though. I shan't do until I've finished my spell of nights,' Vicky explained.

'And then will you want my stuff moved out?'

'No, not on my account. Strictly speaking, the house is still Simon's for the next month.' She paused and gave the younger brother an appraising smile. 'You're not a lot like him, are you?'

'No, he's the brainy one. I prefer communing with nature to sorting out human beings. But we're good mates. He's a decent bloke, is Sime. So come on, tell me about yourself. The unexpurgated version.' He grinned at her engagingly, with something of the charm of his elder brother.

'Even the unexpurgated version wouldn't make the *News of the World*,' returned Vicky with a soft laugh. 'How about you?'

'Me? Oh, I'm a boring sort of bloke. No scandals.

Quite useful, though, for relieving Sime of the occasional clinging vine. For one awful moment there I thought you were Leah,' said Paul, patting his heart and rolling his eyes.

'Who's Leah?'

'Uh-uh. You'll have to ask him about that.'

They continued to chat in a lively, uninhibited fashion, half joking, half serious, both doing their own bit of judicious probing. Vicky learned that Paul's ambition was to have a garden centre of his own eventually, but first he would complete his course on Estate Management.

'It's not my father's idea of a proper career,' he told her. 'Dad had both Simon and me earmarked for the Diplomatic Service, but Simon stuck to his guns about wanting to do medicine, which made it easier for me to do what I wanted. It wasn't popular though.'

'Where did you get your urge to grow things?' Vicky asked. 'From your aunt Lavinia?'

Paul laughed. 'Don't tell me you've already heard about our dear but dotty relative?'

'Yes, I met her yesterday. Simon took me to see her. I thought she was smashing.'

Paul's eyes widened. 'Did he indeed! Quick off the mark introducing you to the family, isn't he? And here was I thinking I might be in with a chance.'

Vicky giggled. 'It's my house, not me, that Simon's after. He'd like to buy it.'

'Yeah, I had heard.' He looked at his watch and sighed. 'Much as I'd love to continue with this riveting conversation, I have to get going—I'm meeting some pals for a bit of canoeing. I just called in to pick up some gear. Would you like to come?' he asked. 'There's a lot going on at the Sports Centre. We could have a meal together afterwards.'

Smiling, she shook her head. 'Thanks for asking, but I have got plans for today.'

'Oh, pity. I'm off on my hols after this, so I shan't be around for a week or two. See you when I get back, I hope. Tell Sime I was here and that I approve the arrangements,' Paul added cheekily.

Having collected the things he needed from the spare room, he departed, waving Vicky a breezy farewell from his metallic green Triumph Convertible.

Left to herself once more, Vicky was free to stir the embers of remembrance, as she had originally intended. She wandered into all the rooms and willed herself back to times past. But the house was now full of other people, Simon Drummond in particular, so that it was reminders of him that confronted her most of the time. His trainers loafing at the bottom of the hall wardrobe, together with a discarded pair of jeans; his fawn leather jacket slung on a peg; his expensive-looking camera hanging by the strap.

Well, that was fine, and she wouldn't be in danger of being haunted by ghosts from the past, as he had suggested. The memories were enshrined in her own heart, the happy ones as well as the sad. As from now she was going to start the rest of her life, free and uncluttered.

She wandered around the sunlit garden, and then

into the garage via the back door. There she found her bicycle, chrome wheels gleaming, tyres hard, brakes working. 'Thanks, Simon,' she murmured with a pleased smile. Idly she tried the front lamp. It worked, as also did the back one. Forgot the batteries, did he? Her smile broadened. Dr Drummond, you certainly are devious! she thought.

She couldn't quite fathom his motive for getting her to stay the night, but whatever it was, she was glad that she had. It had made her more certain that sharing with him, even if only on a temporary basis, could work out satisfactorily for them both. And since she had established with Simon that she would expect to be able to entertain her friends there whenever she liked, that would be very convenient when Tim arrived. She would be able to repay the hospitality which his family had shown to her in Australia. Yes, it looked as if everything was going to work out rather well.

Going to Sunday tea at her aunt's house that afternoon, Vicky was relieved to find that Claire and her family were not expected. It made it easier for her to tell her aunt what had been decided.

Celia was at first openly nonplussed. 'Oh!' she said. 'Oh! Well, I must say I'm rather surprised.'

'I'm a bit surprised myself,' Vicky confessed with a modest laugh. 'He suggested it, just on a short-term basis for the time being, so I've nothing to lose, have I?'

Her aunt sniffed and rubbed her nose with the

back of her hand. 'I suppose you know what you're doing, dear,' she returned, although her manner implied that she had grave doubts about it. 'I don't think your parents would have approved. But I do see you're in an awkward position, this man being who he is.' She sniffed again. 'At least he's not likely to take advantage of you. As a professional man he'll have to behave himself. He'll have his reputation to think of.'

Vicky's uncle Bob put in mildly, 'She'll probably be a darned sight safer with a man about the place than living there on her own. And Claire seemed to think he was a nice enough chap.'

'Why isn't he married, then?' Celia demanded.

'Married to the job, I expect,' said Vicky.

Celia huffed, casting a critical eye over her niece's undeniable appeal; her lissom figure, her bright-eyed vitality. 'Just you be careful, that's all. Even nice men can have a beast within.'

As usual, Bob's sense of the ridiculous brought humour to the proceedings. He growled comically and took a lunge at his wife.

'Not you, silly,' she laughed, 'you're a different generation. Anyway, it's a good thing we didn't say anything to Claire about buying the house for them. If you find it doesn't work out, Vicky, we can always take it from there, can't we?'

It was all much less difficult than Vicky had anticipated. The subject was dropped and she spent a pleasant evening with her relatives, with no recriminations.

* * *

Going in to work on Monday evening, Vicky was thrilled to find herself once more assigned to Coco Ward, where Sister Lorne welcomed her enthusiastically.

'Oh, you're back, Vicky. Cheers!' she said. 'So my moans didn't fall on deaf ears after all.'

Also on nights with Vicky were Staff Nurse Beryl, Jill, a third-year student, and Roxy, a mature auxiliary. All the beds and cots were full, but most of the faces had changed since Vicky was last there. She was, however, glad to see Lisa now out of quarantine and looking a much happier child.

'Yes, she's doing well,' Carole Lorne reported, 'and her father is still visiting, which has helped to keep her spirits up.'

Admitted over the weekend was eleven-year-old Darren. 'He's query appendicitis, and with a history of asthma,' Carole told them. 'His symptoms have subsided for the moment, so it may have been a false alarm. But you'll need to keep your eye on him, he's full of mischief now he feels better.'

Their newest patient was a month-old baby girl, Katy, whose mother had tripped and dropped her that morning.

'There's a sizeable bruise on her forehead, but so far there doesn't appear to be any other damage. Her pupils are normal, so are her vital signs. However, we're to monitor her overnight to be on the safe side. Her mum's staying in, although she isn't breast-feeding. The girl's only seventeen and scared to death, poor kid. She was afraid she might be accused of deliberately hurting the baby, with so much spotlight on child abuse at present, but Casualty were satisfied this was an innocent accident. Do what you can to help the girl,' Carole said. 'Her confidence has been dented.'

Having briefed them on all the other patients, the Sister prepared to leave with the rest of the day staff. 'Adrian said he'd be in again later in case of problems,' she went on, with a swift glance at Beryl. 'Make the most of him, girls. It'll soon be the glorious first of August, then he's off to Leeds, I hear. We shall miss him.'

Beryl nodded, managing a resigned smile. 'Yes, he'd doing Obstetrics and Gynae first, then a GP course.'

Being a comparative newcomer on the staff, Vicky had been content to listen, but she remarked now, 'Thank goodness the registrars don't change every six months as well. At least there's some continuity.' And in her heart she couldn't help wondering what Simon's long-term plans were.

The night nurses scattered to their duties, straightening cots and beds, checking infusions, maintaining fluid charts, giving a cuddle here and there, and doing the myriad tasks that were necessary before the ward lights could be dimmed and peace reigned.

The few late visitors had left by this time and there only remained Hazel, Baby Katy's mother, who was to sleep in the baby's cubicle. With a persistent plaintive wail coming from that direction, Vicky deposited a collection of toys back in the play area, washed her hands and went to see if all was well.

She found the young mother, a well-built teenager in skin-tight jeans, hovering uncertainly by the cot.

'Everything all right, Hazel?' Vicky asked kindly. 'She's due a feed, isn't she?'

The girl nodded, smoothing back her long, lank brown hair and throwing a timid glance in Vicky's direction. 'Y-yes. Is that OK? I-I'm almost scared to pick her up.'

Vicky smiled encouragement. 'You'll get used to handling her. It's just a question of experience. Shall we change her nappy first? And I'll check her temperature while we're about it.'

Chatting in a quietly confident manner, Vicky slipped a gown over her pink uniform, lifted up the mewling infant and made soothing noises for a few moments.

'Have you got any children?' the girl asked, envying Vicky's easy handling of the baby.

'No. Probably if ever I did have I'd be useless,' Vicky laughed. 'Every time they sneezed I'd be imagining the worst! Ignorance is bliss sometimes.'

She laid the infant gently back in her cot and used the occasion to show the best way to go about things, letting the young mother do the work. There was nothing abnormal about the soiled nappy and the baby's temperature showed no cause for concern.

'That's fine,' Vicky reassured the girl. 'Now you sit down and give her a cuddle, and I'll get her bottle for you.'

Stripping off her gown, Vicky washed her hands again and went to the kitchen to get the pre-packed milk feed. She stayed for a few minutes to see the girl comfortably settled and the baby sucking contentedly, and promised to come back later.

Roxy and Jill were still busy in the sluice. Beryl was sorting through case notes in the office with Adrian. Vicky, taking a last tour around the darkened ward, thought she heard a muffled sob. It came from the farthest corner of one of the six-bedded bays. Shining her torch, she discovered eight-year-old Sally with her head under the bedclothes, sobbing. Sally was due for a cystogram the following day to investigate a bladder infection.

'What's the matter, sweetheart?' Vicky asked. 'Have you got a pain?'

The child shook her head, still sobbing. 'I c-can't find my bunny—and I d-don't like the dark. M-Mummy always lets me have a light.'

'Oh dear! Well, let's see what we can do.' Vicky switched on the shaded green bedlight. 'There you are—that's better, isn't it? There's nothing to be frightened of. Now, where's your bunny got to?' She searched around and found the missing threadbare toy at the bottom of the bed. 'Here he is. All right now? We shall be here all the time, and you can see us in the light over the desk, can't you? Close your eyes and go to sleep now. It'll soon be morning. Night-night, Sally.'

Darren's bed, the first one in the same bay, was still empty, Vicky noted. She had glimpsed the eleven-year-old nipping off towards the toilets when she had collected the baby's feed. She decided it was time he was back and went to check that he was not in trouble. Although there were no locks on any of the lavatory doors one of them was closed. Was that her imagination, or could she see a thin wisp of smoke rising over the top?

'Darren?' she called. 'Are you all right in there?'

'Yeah, just coming.' There was a pause, the sound of the cistern being flushed, then the lad sauntered out, hitching up his cotton pyjamas. He was breathing a trifle heavily. 'I'm not a kid, y'know. I can see to myself,' he said with a sheepish grin.

'I wondered if you were feeling sick again.' Vicky gave him a long straight look. 'Have you been smoking? Because if you have you deserve to feel sick.'

'Me, miss? No, miss,' he returned, looking the picture of innocence.

She was not altogether convinced. She glanced into the cubicle but saw no obvious signs of smoking. 'OK,' she said, 'but you're puffing like an old billy-goat. You sound as if you need your Intal. Have you got a spinhaler by your bed?'

'Yes, miss.' Darren sighed with exaggerated patience.

'All right, wash your hands and go back to bed. I'll be with you in a minute.' *And when I come I shall take a look in your locker, young man,* Vicky decided warily.

She left him industriously washing his hands while

she went to see that Baby Katy had taken her feed and been properly winded before being put back in her cot.

'She didn't want it all,' Hazel told her, 'and she puked a bit.'

'Well, that's nothing to worry about. She seems contented, doesn't she? Tuck her down on her side, and if you put a rolled nappy behind her, like this, she won't be in danger of getting on to her back. Now, why don't you get ready for bed yourself?' Vicky suggested kindly. 'You can make a drink in the parents' rest-room if you want one. And if Katy needs a feed in the night, there's no need for you to get up. We'll see to it for you.'

She left the baby's cubicle just as Darren, with a scream of terror, ran from the children's toilets. Vicky saw with horror that there was a bright flame licking from the pocket of his pyjama jacket. Instinctively she blocked his frenzied flight. Wrestling the boy to the ground, she threw herself on top of him, smothering the fire with her own body.

And that was the sight which greeted Simon Drummond coming in search of Adrian to see whether any matters of importance had arisen in his absence.

With a muttered oath he stripped off his jacket as he ran to Vicky's aid. Dropping it over both nurse and boy, he packed it firmly around them. But Vicky was scarcely aware of his presence as she realised with stupendous relief that there was no more searing heat. The flames had been extinguished.

'It's all right, pet,' she soothed, trying to calm the hysterical youngster, 'it's all right. You're safe now—the fire's out.'

CHAPTER SEVEN

THE INCIDENT on Coco Ward remained a talking point among the night nurses for some time. It certainly bonded them together as they faced the need to be constantly alert where their young patients were concerned.

'I'm glad I wasn't first on the scene,' Jill said, taking her coffee break with Vicky the following night. The third-year student eyed her senior with due respect. 'I don't know whether I could have done what you did.'

'Oh, I'm sure you could,' Vicky returned, dismissing her own presence of mind as the norm. 'It's a gut reaction really, a spur-of-the-moment thing.' She took a bite of her chocolate biscuit before adding, 'You just get on with it.'

'Weren't you afraid of getting burnt?'

'No, I didn't think about it. Anyway, it wasn't a big fire—only might have been.' Nevertheless, a chill crept over her skin as her thoughts went back to that first shock-filled moment and the acrid smell of burning cloth.

Vicky had been vaguely aware that within seconds there were feet hurrying to her assistance, but by then the immediate danger was past. Sitting back on her heels when she had felt it safe to do so, she found herself looking into the concerned face of Simon, squatting on the floor beside her. Around them was a ring of other anxious faces, including the Night Nursing Officer who had been on her way to make her rounds at the time. Then someone helped Vicky to her feet while others hastened to take care of Darren. She remembered Simon's terse enquiry, 'You all right?' before he had ordered Roxy to take her away and look after her.

Miraculously her prompt action had saved the boy from serious burns. This time there was no call for the urgent, life-saving measures which had been necessary in the case of young Hannah, who Vicky had escorted to East Grinstead. Priority of treatment was for the acute broncho-spasm brought on by the fright which Darren had suffered. It took the application of a Ventolin nebuliser to relieve his distressed breathing before his superficial chest burns could be dressed, and a few pointed questions asked.

Investigating Darren's charred pyjama jacket, they had discovered the cause of the fire—a half-smoked cigarette and a half-burnt booklet of matches in the remains of the pocket. It came to light that he had cadged them from his fourteen-year-old brother who had visited him that afternoon.

'Oh dear! Boys will be boys,' the Nursing Officer sighed, filling out an incident form when the fuss had died down. 'You need eyes in the back of your head with some of 'em. We must be thankful he didn't set fire to the hospital as well!'

She seemed satisfied that no blame whatever

attached to the staff, but Vicky could have kicked herself for not following up her suspicions more closely.

'I did wonder if he'd been smoking,' she said, 'but I thought he'd probably flushed the thing down the loo, not put a live stub in his pocket on top of matches, the silly noodle!'

Vicky herself had come to no harm, apart from a slight reddening at the base of her hand, scorch marks on her tabard, a hole in the knee of her tights, and feeling generally like a limp lettuce. Her state of mind wasn't helped when Simon came to find her after dealing with the boy. His keen eyes slid over her where she sat in the kitchen, sipping the coffee that Roxy had made for her and trying to appear composed, although finding it difficult to stop her hands from trembling.

'Darren's OK, you'll be glad to hear,' Simon told her with an understanding smile. 'He'll be sore for a few days, but nothing much more than that. How are you?' Taking the mug from her hands, he turned them over and inspected the palms. 'Mmm—just a bit toasted there, but you'll survive.'

His caring touch made her colour rise. Her mouth dried and her heart began drumming painfully. 'Which is more than can be said for my tights!' she found the breath to say. Pulling her hands away, she showed him the hole more to avoid the disturbing physical impact than because she was bothered about the damage. 'Look at that! New on tonight, they were.'

'Oh dear!' Slowly he trailed a finger around the

edges of the tear in the black nylons. 'Too bad!' Then he caught her eye and murmured impishly, 'But fortunately tights are replaceable. My housemate wouldn't have been.'

They exchanged grins, and Vicky was glad that for the moment they were alone. 'Shush!' she warned. 'You'll set all the tongues wagging.'

'My dear child,' Simon replied, 'if I bothered about wagging tongues I'd be a nervous wreck by now. It's bound to come out sooner of later that we're sharing a house. I suppose you'll be needing a hand with your luggage before long?' he went on.

'I'll let you know if I do. And I am *not* your dear child, Dr Drummond.'

Folding his arms, he studied her with a disarming smile. 'Slip of the tongue, Miss Chalfont. You'll get used to my funny little ways.'

'You might find yourself having to get used to mine,' she returned.

'I'm well aware of that, but with a bit of give and take I expect we shall manage.'

The Nursing Officer, joining them to enquire how Vicky was feeling, brought an end to their exchange. 'Full marks for keeping your head, Nurse,' she said. 'Now, I think you should go and freshen up a bit—and then it would be a good idea if you took your meal break. That'll give you a chance to get yourself together, won't it?' she added kindly. 'You look a bit frayed around the edges. Not surprising, in the circumstances.'

Vicky needed no encouragement to excuse herself. If she was looking frazzled it had less to do with

Darren's accident than the effect of five minutes under the close scrutiny of the charismatic registrar. But that must have been because it came on top of the accident, she explained it away to herself. At least, she hoped that was the reason, or it was going to be an emotional disaster when it came to living under the same roof as the man, bumping into him when she least expected it and so forth. Thank goodness Tim would be on the horizon shortly, which would give her something else to think about.

At report the next evening Carole told them that it appeared Darren had been smoking regularly since the age of ten. In fact the whole family were smokers. 'The kind of people no amount of counselling can help,' she sighed. 'We're just here to pick up the pieces later. His mother did apologise for her other son's stupidity, but on the whole they all seemed to think it was something of a laugh.'

There being no recurrence of his appendicitis symptoms, Darren had been discharged to the care of his own GP.

Baby Katy was also discharged after showing no further ill effects from being dropped, and the Health Visitor was contacted to give the baby's mother any support she might need.

The remainder of Vicky's time on nights passed uneventfully, at least where their small patients were concerned. There were no emergencies and Simon's presence was not required during the night, about which she didn't know whether she was glad or sorry. Adrian, on the other hand, was a regular visitor and Beryl only too delighted to see him. But as the day of his departure for Leeds drew nearer she grew more and more despondent.

'He's promised we'll still keep in touch,' she confided to Vicky, 'but it's miles to Yorkshire, isn't it? I suppose I could always get myself a job up there, except that—I wouldn't want him to think I was running after him.' She shrugged. 'Oh, I don't know what to do. I mean, he's attractive, isn't he? He's bound to get involved with someone else.'

In her heart, Beryl knew she had already lost Adrian. If, indeed, she had ever had him, Vicky thought sympathetically. She felt like telling the girl she was better off without him, but that wouldn't have helped since Beryl was so infatuated with the SHO.

'Yes, I know Adrian's got a lot going for him,' Vicky agreed, 'but so have you, Beryl. Don't underrate yourself. I should wait a bit and see how things work out before you do anything drastic.'

Meantime, there was the End-of-Firm party to look forward to; the farewell gig held in the doctors' mess at six-monthly intervals before all the housemen changed their jobs and went off to other parts of the country. Vicky was pleased she would be off nights by then. It would be her first social occasion at Wealdwood. She expected Simon would be there, and since she would be moving in with him the following day, it would get them off to a nice informal beginning.

There was a rising tide of excitement within her at the prospect, but she dismissed that as a natural reaction to an unpredictable experiment. She had already packed most of her belongings in readiness for the move. How to get them over to the house was another matter.

It went against the grain to ask for Simon's help since, in a way, she was already beholden to him. When they had first talked matters through that evening in the kitchen she had raised the question of money, but he had swept aside her suggestion that his rent ought to be reduced accordingly.

'No, you can be my guest for now,' he had insisted. 'We'll talk about it again at the end of my present contract.'

Now it seemed important to establish her independence, even if only in small matters. Good of him, of course, to offer to move her, but she didn't want to be any further indebted to him. Vicky decided to ask Anna to help, or failing that, get a taxi.

Before reporting for her last night of duty she phoned her aunt Celia, to bring her up to date with things.

'Oh, I am glad you rang, dear,' Celia said. 'We had a caller yesterday afternoon. A friend of yours, Tim—just arrived here from Sydney, he told us. Well, I couldn't get in touch with you at the time, and he couldn't stop—he was on his way to his grandparents at Westgate. But he wants to see you, so he's going to ring here again. I'll give him your home number next time, shall I?'

'Yes, please, if you would,' Vicky returned enthusiastically. 'I used to work with Tim over there—he was one of the charge nurses on my floor.'

'He seemed a very pleasant young man,' her aunt prattled on. 'He was driving an Escort which he'd hired at Heathrow. Your uncle lent him a road map and gave him directions to where he wanted to go, but I doubt whether he needed them. He managed to find his way to us all right.' Celia paused for breath. 'He obviously thinks a lot of you. Is he . . . more than just a friend?'

Vicky chuckled. 'Now, now, Celia, don't start romancing! He's a friend, and that's all.'

'Oh! And I'd already got your uncle lined up to give you away.'

Vicky laughed again. 'When that time comes, if ever, I promise I shall want Uncle Bob to do the honours.'

When all their young patients were settled that night the staff of Coco Ward relaxed with a cup of coffee for a few moments. Gathered in the office, their quiet talk centred on the forthcoming changeover of the housemen.

'At least on Paeds we get SHOs,' said Roxy, 'not new boys green behind the ears who think they know it all.'

The others murmured in agreement, thinking of the young doctors who would shortly be arriving to pursue the next stage in the course of their careers. The twice-yearly upheaval was guaranteed to bring groans from the nursing staff whose lot it was to cope with the fresh personnel. It often required a degree of diplomacy where some of the doctors were concerned.

Beryl was very subdued, brooding over the fact of losing Adrian. Jill, also parting from one of the housemen she had been dating, was more vocally mournful. Apart from decrying the general chaos, both Vicky and Roxy accepted the inevitable as a fact of hospital life, but they all agreed it wasn't the easiest of times.

The following morning Vicky was a little late off duty, staying to feather-braid Lisa's long dark hair for her. Although still on antibiotics, she was now making a good recovery and presented a totally different picture from the feverish, desperately ill child whom Vicky had first seen.

Today was Lisa's birthday. Later on there would be a surprise birthday cake, and greetings over the hospital radio, and a small present from the stock of toys which Carole kept especially for such occasions.

'So what's all this in aid of?' teased Vicky, finishing off the plait with a red ribbon bow. 'Anything special happening today?'

Lisa giggled. 'You know what it is. I'm ten today.'

'Oh, yes, I do remember hearing something about it. Happy birthday, pet. Sorry I shall have to miss your party—I shall be asleep. Anyway, have a lovely day. See you again soon.'

She waved the excited youngster goodbye, collected her things from the staff room and went to take her leave of Carole.

'You coming to the beano tonight?' Carole asked.

'Yes, I thought I would,' Vicky said, 'although I won't know many people there.'

'Simon told me Sir James hopes to be able to make it. You haven't met our consultant yet, have you Vicky? He's been convalescing after a bout of pneumonia. Not that we ever see him a great deal these days. And Simon runs things perfectly well without him anyway.' The Sister paused and gave her staff nurse an enquiring glance. 'Simon also mentioned that you're following up my idea—about sharing your house with him.'

To her embarrassment Vicky found herself blushing. 'Well, yes, it seems the best solution to date,' she admitted with a shy smile. 'We'll have to see how it goes.'

Preening herself, Carole breathed on her nails and polished them on her uniform. 'There you are! I told you I was a genius, didn't I?'

Vicky laughed. 'Time will tell,' she said. So Simon was was already spreading the word, was he? He was certainly living up to his boast about not giving a toss what people thought, she reflected.

Vicky slept well until five o'clock that afternoon. Then she showered and went along in her white towelling bathrobe to see if Anna was in.

Only just off duty herself, Anna was ridding her uniform of watch, badges, etcetera, before putting it in her laundry bag. 'Hi!' she exclaimed with a pleased smile. 'Where've you been lately? I was beginning to wonder if you'd gone back to Oz. And with all this rumpus about what's happening to the Health Service I wouldn't have blamed you.'

'No, nothing like that, just nights,' Vicky said, smiling. She came to sit on the side of her friend's bed. 'Anyway, I was homesick for England. Funny things, roots.'

The girls had not seen each other since their meditative walk in the country. Anna made coffee and they sat and caught up with each other's news.

Anna's neatly plucked eyebrows shot up when Vicky revealed her plans. 'You're moving in with him? Who suggested that?'

'Simon did.'

'Oh, did he?' Anna looked amused. 'What goes on between you two?'

Vicky chuckled. 'Sweet nothing, I can assure you. This is purely a matter of convenience. Simon's boxing clever. He's hoping to keep me sweet so I'll agree to sell to him in the end, I expect.'

'Hmm! If you say so. But no guy's going to agree to share with a girl—for whatever reason—unless he likes her company. Well, just say when you want to move your stuff and we'll do it. I'd quite like to see your house, anyway.'

'Thanks, pal,' said Vicky. 'Some time tomorrow? There's not really time today, before the party. You are going, aren't you?'

'Yeah.' With a selfconscious grin, Anna ran a hand through her spiky fair hair. 'I've got a kind of date—with Ben Milden,' she said.

'What do you mean, *kind of*?' Vicky asked, intrigued.

'We-ell, I got talking to him in the Swan the other night. There were just the two of us, and he asked me back to his rooms for a nightcap. And we played records, and Scrabble, and talked some more. And he said he'd look forward to seeing me at the party. He's really nice, Vict,' Anna went on. 'I've never had a chance to get to know him before.'

Vicky was thrilled for Anna who was something of a loner herself. 'Yes, I've always liked Ben,' she said. 'Oh, but you're going to be leaving here soon! Oh, what a pity you didn't get together sooner.'

Anna wrinkled her nose. 'Mmm, but it'll be another three months yet. And Ben hopes to be moving to Guy's at the end of the year, so that could work out quite well. Anyway, the future can look after itself. This makes life interesting for the present, doesn't it?' she said, optimistically.

Decorated with balloons and streamers, the doctors' mess was looking suitably festive for the farewell celebrations. It was a warm night. Windows were open, and the pulsating beat of disco music welcomed party-goers from all departments of the hospital.

In Australia there had been plenty of opportunity for wearing lightweight summer frocks, so that for tonight Vicky had no difficulty in finding something suitable for the temperature. She chose a low-waisted sea-green voile dress with narrow ribbon shoulder straps, and she bunched her dark hair up on top with a matching ribbon. The style gave emphasis to her classic heart-shaped features. The warm amber-brown eyes that looked back at her from the mirror were bright with vitality, and there was a certain glow about her as she fastened a fine gold chain around her slim neck.

Anna, too, looked becoming in a simple black sleeveless dress with which she wore a long rope of pearls and large pendant earrings.

At nine o'clock the crowd was reaching capacity when the two girls arrived. Searching for faces they knew, they caught sight of Ben and waved to him. His rather solemn, owlish face brightened as he threaded his way through the crowd to reach them.

'Hallo, you two. What kept you?' he said. 'Come over to the bar and have some refreshment. What would you like?'

There was a momentary pause in the music while a tape was being changed and for a time conversation became possible at a normal level.

Presently they were also joined by Carole and her husband, Greville, the neuro-surgical consultant.

'So you're still with us, are you, Vicky, in spite of the old country going to the dogs?' Greville remarked.

She laughed. 'Yes, I'm still here, although don't ask me why.'

'Your propensity for lame ducks, I expect. It's a national failing. It's what keeps us all with our noses to the grindstone,' the consultant observed. 'Anna, my dear, what's this I hear about you wanting to desert us? We *need* you.'

Anna laughed and shook her head. 'Nobody's that indispensable. I'm looking after Number One lame duck—me! Either that, or I'll end up in one of your beds.'

'Heigh-ho!' the neuro consultant sighed in mock despair. 'No staying power, some of you youngsters.'

'Listen to Methuselah!' mocked Carole.

Dancing had begun again and Vicky found herself being whisked into the action by a very exuberant Adrian, who appeared out of the blue.

'At last!' he exclaimed, whirling her round and pulling her close. 'My first chance to get to grips with you. You've wasted your opportunities, you know. We could have had a ball over the past few weeks.'

Vicky laughed. 'There'll be a whole new field of talent waiting for you up North, Adrian.' She paused. 'Isn't Beryl here tonight?'

'Yeah, she's around, but I'm out of favour for the moment. All I did was spend a little time with one of the theatre girls. Women!'

'Good for Beryl. You know you're a swine, don't you?' Vicky said lightly. 'For the life of me I don't know why she puts up with you.'

'You don't? Then maybe I should complete your education while there's still time.' Adrian nuzzled his cheek against hers, murmuring, 'You're a very cuddlesome little thing, aren't you?'

A tap on his shoulder unexpectedly cut short his advances. A deep voice broke in, 'Excuse me!' and Simon came between them and took Vicky into his own arms.

'Hey!' Adrian protested. 'What's all this about?'

Simon replied blithely, 'Sir James is over at the

bar and he'd like to talk to you.' He danced off with Vicky, saying, 'As a matter of fact, I thought you looked as though you needed rescuing. Did you?'

'Not really,' Vicky laughed. 'I can handle Adrian. But whether she could handle Simon was less than certain. Part of her was annoyed, thinking what a nerve he had breaking them up like that, while another part was flattered that he had done so. The trouble was that finding herself in his arms seemed to rob her of the power to think straight. All she knew was how irresistibly seductive those arms were, how much her inner self clamoured to be held even more closely against his virile, powerful body.

With a supreme effort she subdued her heady desires and said with a bright smile, 'I haven't told you—I met your brother the other morning.'

'No, but he did.' Simon's enquiring eyes sought hers. 'Well?'

'Fine!' she returned. 'We hit it off immediately. And I learned all your family secrets.'

'Oh, you did, did you?' He curbed a smile while his fingers exerted a gentle pressure against her ribs. It sent a delightful thrill through her body, and she squirmed and laughed.

'You mustn't believe all my young brother says,' Simon told her. 'He talks off the top of his head sometimes.'

'I can believe that. He was quite complimentary about you,' she cracked.

'Ah, that must have been one of his more lucid moments. Thank goodness he's away for the next couple of weeks. At least we shall be left in peace while you move in. When is that to be?'

'Tomorrow evening, I thought. Anna's going to drive me over.'

Simon frowned. 'What made you ask Anna? I told you I'd do it.'

'Yes, I know you did, and thanks for offering, but—um—well,' Vicky floundered, not knowing quite how to explain matters, 'I—I didn't know when it would be convenient for you, did I? And Anna said she'd like to see the house, so . . .'

'Oh!' He sounded aggrieved, like a small boy robbed of a treat. 'She can see the house any time, can't she?' Nearby, Anna and Ben were dancing together, gazing soulfully into each other's eyes, and Simon went on gruffly, 'By the look of it, I should think Anna's going to be much too busy to run around after you.'

Vicky looked, and smiled. She was amused by his attitude. 'Friends don't renege on promises,' she returned.

'Exactly. And I said I'd do it. Or don't you count me a friend?'

His full, shapely lips were set in a stern, disapproving line, and she couldn't help the small trill of laughter which bubbled to her throat. 'I'd like to think you were. But, Simon, does it really matter who does it? I mean,' she shrugged, 'as far as that goes, suppose you got caught up at the hospital after you'd made arrangements with me? Anyway, it's all fixed now, but I did appreciate your offer. No offence, honestly.'

He said no more. His lips gradually softened.

They grinned at each other and, impulsively, Vicky reached up and kissed his cheek. 'Friends?'

'I'll consider it.'

'Oh dear,' she sighed, 'if we're going to fall out before we've even started, perhaps it's not such a good idea after all, me moving in.'

'Rubbish!' Simon retorted. 'All relationships have teething troubles. Think of this as cutting your first incisor.' He began to guide her off the floor. 'Now you might as well come and meet Sir James while you've got the chance. The more people you know in this business the better. I've a great admiration for the fellow. Unfortunately he hasn't been too well lately. I shouldn't be surprised if he decided to retire before long.'

Vicky did recall seeing something of Sir James Latimer in the old days, but she'd had no personal dealings with him. Now he seemed leaner than before—a tall, grey-haired man with a deep forehead and a sweet expression. Elegantly dressed, his light grey suit hung loosely on him and his crisp white shirt was easy about the collar. He stood with Adrian, Carole and her husband, talking in a pleasantly modulated, slightly husky voice.

Introducing Vicky, Simon said, 'She's just returned to home base after trying her wings abroad.'

'Where was that?' Sir James enquired politely, extending a well-kept hand to shake hers.

'Sydney,' Vicky told him. 'I enjoyed every minute of it, but it's lovely to be back.'

'East, west, home's best?' queried Sir James with a twinkle. 'Well, that at least is encouraging to hear in these beleaguered times. Let's hope you won't be tempted to fly away again.'

There followed a lively discussion on the malaise in the Health Service; understaffing and underfunding of hospitals, growing waiting lists, and the tardiness of the bureaucrats in facing up to the problem.

'At least the Friends of Wealdwood have done their bit,' Greville said. 'I see our Scanner Appeal has topped the target, thanks to the countless people who made an effort, bless 'em.'

'Yes, I never cease to be amazed at the way society will respond to a worthwhile cause. It's most uplifting,' Sir James returned.

Simon was bleeped and went away to the telephone, and Vicky seized the chance to move on and greet other people she knew.

In fact she discovered that her circle of friends, even in the short time she'd been back, was wider than she'd realised. While working in Casualty she had brushed shoulders with many departments, and her own outgoing disposition ensured a warm welcome from her contacts.

Inevitably, some of the nurses she talked to wanted to hear about her experiences in Australia and whether the life there was as good as it purported to be.

'Oh yes, it's terrific,' Vicky enthused. 'Over there you're a Sister as soon as you're trained, although there are grades of seniority, of course. And there are some fantastic new medical centres opening up all over the place. People mostly live out in rented units. Then there's all that gorgeous weather, and the beaches, and the Aussies certainly know how to enjoy it. The trouble is,' she sighed, 'it's such a long way from here.'

'Too true,' mourned one of the girls. 'I don't think I could go unless I had the fare home safely tucked away.'

Sir James was right, Vicky found herself brooding. Home was where your heart was—or something like that—except that her own heart was totally unreliable at present, not knowing where it wanted to be. For instance, it was ridiculous the way her eyes kept searching the room for a missing blond head when she should be concentrating on present company. With an effort she turned her attention back to her companions and answered their questions as best she could.

As the night wore on and barriers melted, there were many affectionate goodbyes to departing housemen. When the bar closed at midnight some couples slipped away to continue their leavetaking in more private surroundings.

Simon had not come back to the party. Sir James and Carole and her husband had long since departed. Vicky had seen Beryl go off with Adrian's arm around her, and Anna and Ben—about to leave together—came over to see if they could walk Vicky back to the Nurses' Home.

'No, I'm fine,' she smiled. 'June and Maddy are coming back to my room for a coffee.'

'OK, I'm on a half-day tomorrow, so any time after lunch I'm yours,' Anna promised.

'Thanks, I'm all packed and ready.'

Vicky collected her long scarf from one of the coat-hooks and joined the other two nurses. They wandered back to the Nurses' Home, speculating on what the new breed of housemen would be like. After a relaxed half-hour in Vicky's room, gossiping over their drinks, her friends left and she prepared for bed.

Usually Vicky read for a while before putting out the light, but tonight she lay there thinking, wondering yet again whether she was about to embark on the most stupid episode of her life.

It was something like putting her head into the lion's mouth, she mused, smiling to herself at the simile. In a way Simon was rather leonine, with his bold, beautiful head, his lean muscular hips and his leisured stride. In spite of what he had said about being a reasonable man, he was far more complex than might first appear. Dr Simon Drummond was no pushover; he was a very determined character, not given to being thwarted.

Vicky sighed heavily and wished he were not so devastatingly attractive. Thank goodness Tim would soon be around to claim her attention. She almost couldn't wait for him to phone her.

Tim was good-looking too, in his own robust sort of fashion. That would show Dr Drummond that she wasn't just there waiting to be twisted around his little finger!

She put out the light and spent her last waking moments wondering what incident had called him from the party.

CHAPTER EIGHT

THE SKY was as brilliantly blue as a travel brochure. Through half-closed eyes Vicky idly watched an enormous bumble-bee buzzing around a tall pink hollyhock.

Anna roused herself sufficiently to take a drink of orange juice from the tall glass beside her on the lawn. 'This is the life! Who wants to be a millionaire? I do!' she said.

The two girls were relaxing in deck chairs in the back garden of Vicky's house after having moved her belongings from the Nurses' Home.

'I could settle for a sugar daddy, an account at Harrods and a yacht on the Côte d'Azur or somewhere,' Anna went on, readjusting her sunglasses.

Vicky laughed and stretched lazily, letting her summer sandals slip off her bare feet. 'You'd be bored out of your skull in no time. Anyway, what about Ben? I thought you were all geared to take off into the sunset with him? He's a great guy, but an account with M & S would be more his style.'

'Don't rush me,' Anna said serenely, 'we're just good mates so far. But I'm a rotten sailor, so I might manage without the yacht.' She grinned and glanced at her watch. 'Have to leave you now, I'm afraid, much as I'd love to stay. He's taking me to Hever Castle tonight—there's a production of *A Midsummer Night's Dream* in the gardens there.'

'Well, you couldn't have a more romantic setting than that, so watch it.' Vicky wriggled her toes back into her sandals and went with Anna to where her car was parked.

'You watch it too,' warned Anna. 'Holed up in this place with that sex symbol? There's an explosive situation if ever I saw one!'

'Phooey!' Vicky scoffed. 'Once the novelty's over he'll hardly know I'm here. All that concerns him is that I'll let him stay put. Now if I were an interesting case of scoliosis or something it might be different. Thanks for your help. Have a good time.' She waved Anna goodbye and went back to the garden to collect their used glasses.

In the kitchen on the table was the small carton containing the odds and ends of groceries she had accumulated during her stay at the Nurses' Home. These she put away in cupboard and fridge, at the same time taking note of the stock already there. Simon was amply supplied with everything, and probably kept replenished by his home help, Vicky surmised. But since she could hardly dip into his provisions until they came to some sort of arrangement, she decided to shoot down to the local shopping parade for a few more things of her own.

Upon her return, she was putting her bicycle back in the garage when a white Ford Escort cruised to a halt outside the gate. Her face lit with pleasure as she saw Tim emerge from the driving seat and stand there for a moment, hitching up his light blue stone-washed jeans while he surveyed the house.

'Tim!' she yelled, bounding down the path to greet him.

A brilliant smile creased his amiable, longish face. He held out his arms to her and they embraced. 'Hi, Pommie! I made it!'

'So you did,' she said, smiling back. 'I'd been waiting for a phone call. How did you know where to find me?'

'Your aunt briefed me. A great communicator, your auntie. I hope nobody ever entrusts her with any State secrets.'

Vicky laughed. 'She knew I was looking forward to seeing you. Come on in.' Tucking her arm through his, she led him towards the house. 'Where've you been, and where are you off to now?' she wanted to know. 'Can you stay for a few days? I'm not working until Saturday, and there's a spare room here . . .'

'Sounds good to me!' Laughter lines creased the corners of his deep-set eyes. 'I was hoping you'd ask. But what about this guy you're living with? Will it be all right with him?'

'Yes, of course,' Vicky said, 'we sorted that out before I moved in, and I'm not *living with him* in that sense; it is my house. This arrangement is just temporary—it's convenient for both of us for the time being.'

Tim nodded wisely, a dimple flickering in his cheek. 'I'm well-informed as to the set-up. Your aunt's none too happy about it, I would have you know.'

She chuckled. 'Celia hasn't moved into the twentieth century yet, but her heart's in the right place.'

She found him a can of larger—Simon's, but she would replace it later—and they sat on the patio in the late afternoon sunshine, talking as though they hadn't seen each other for years.

Reminiscing, Vicky said, 'It's barely a couple of months since I left Sydney, you know. Seems longer than that, really.'

Tim sighed extravagantly. 'Yes, more like a couple of years. We all miss you, Vicky. Especially me.'

The warmth in his eyes made her feel slightly embarrassed. She laughed and said, 'I'm sure you didn't come all this way to tell me that. Why did you decide to come?'

'Oh, I had some holiday allowance to use up. Plus, I'm starting a new job when I go back. DON of a small community hospital.' He went on to describe it to her.

'It sounds terrific, Tim. You *are* moving up. Fantastic!'

'Yes, I'm looking forward to it.' He hesitated. 'When are you coming back? You could always join me.'

Again she caught an expression in his eyes which was somewhat disquieting. She had known that he liked her, and the feeling was mutual, but that was as far as it went where she was concerned. Now she said, 'Oh, I don't know, Tim. One day perhaps, but not in the immediate future.' She smiled at him.

'Anyway, there are more important things to talk about now. Like, what shall we do tomorrow? Would you like to see Canterbury Cathedral?'

He reached over to ruffle her dark, silky hair. 'I've done Canterbury. My grandparents took me there.'

'What d'you mean, you've *done* Canterbury?' Vicky demanded. 'That's centuries of history you're talking about!'

'What I didn't come all this way for was a history lesson,' he returned. 'I came to see you.'

'No, you didn't. At least, not only me. And you ought to see as much of the country as you can while you're here.' She chewed her thumbnail thoughtfully. 'I know, what about a bit of local colour while the weather's nice? There's a hop farm I could take you to, not too far away. You can see how some people used to spend their summer holidays in the olden days. Whole families used to go hop-picking—it was often the only taste of the countryside they got. All mechanised now, of course, and the oasthouses are listed buildings. It's interesting; you'd enjoy it.'

'I'll enjoy whatever in your company,' Tim said gallantly. 'I have to leave here early on Saturday, though—loads of people to see. Next I'm booked to visit my mum's sister in Brussels.'

'Fine, that gives us three whole days,' Vicky enthused. 'We can spend some time in London, and perhaps go to one of the historic houses around here. There's a lot to see in Kent.'

They were talking about what they would do that evening when Vicky heard a key in the front door.

'That'll be Simon,' she said, jumping up from her chair with a fluttery feeling in her throat. She wished that she could have told Simon in advance about Tim's visit, but here he was, so that was that. 'I only moved in this afternoon,' she explained to Tim, 'so I'd better go and show myself. Come and meet him.'

She left him to follow while she went through into the hall to where Simon stood glancing through his post which she had picked up and put on the hall table.

He was minus jacket and tie and his dark blue shirt was open at the neck. He looked warm and a little weary, but when he glanced up to see her, he said, cheerfully enough, 'I gathered you'd arrived,' and nodded towards her suitcases which stood at the foot of the stairs. 'Everything OK?' His glance strayed beyond her to where Tim had by now appeared, framed in the doorway of the lounge. 'Oh! We have a visitor?'

'Yes, Simon,' Vicky began, feeling oddly ill at ease, 'this is Tim, a friend of mine from Sydney . . .'

The two men shook hands, each weighing the other up while they exchanged polite greetings.

Vicky went on over-brightly, 'Tim's staying until Saturday. That is all right with you, isn't it? I mean, you weren't expecting anyone yourself, were you?'

'No, fine. I'll let you know if and when I am,' Simon returned. 'Well, don't let me interrupt your reunion. I must go and change.'

Was it her imagination, or did she sense a touch of frost in his manner? 'Oh, do come and have a drink with us first,' she coaxed. 'Has it been a heavy day?'

'So-so,' he shrugged. 'My clinic seemed to go on forever. All right, what are you drinking?'

'Tim's drinking your lager.'

'Oh, is he? Well, I won't join you in that, Tim, I may have to go back to the hospital tonight,' Simon replied. 'I'll have some spa water and orange juice, Vicky, please.'

She hastened into the kitchen to get it, eager to make everything agreeable. When she returned with the long drink, clinking with ice, both men were chatting easily on the patio, with Simon offering to show Tim around the hospital if he so wished.

'Thanks, Vicky.' Simon took the glass from her and smiled at their visitor. 'Well trained, isn't she? And I haven't even started on her yet.'

Vicky rolled her eyes. 'Talk like that and you'll get the next lot over you!' she promised.

Tim chuckled. 'That's what I've been missing since she left us—the quick riposte. Worth coming halfway round the world for.'

Simon's astute gaze slid from Tim to her and back again. 'And what are your plans, having come?' he asked.

'He's spending the next three days with me,' Vicky put in, 'then he's got oodles of other people to see. Tonight I thought I'd take him to an olde-English pub for a meal. Why don't you come too, Simon?'

He shook his head. 'Too busy. You go off and enjoy yourselves.'

'I'd better smarten up a bit, then. I'll get my stuff.' Tim went out to his car to collect his luggage.

'Shall I take these up for you?' Simon picked up Vicky's cases and carried them upstairs.

'Thank you,' she said, following him, wanting to explain properly about her unexpected visitor. 'Simon, I'm really sorry to have sprung this on you so soon,' she went on as he dropped the bags outside her bedroom door. 'Tim simply turned up out of the blue, or I would have let you know beforehand.'

His magnetic blue eyes smiled directly into hers; mind-blowing, making her feel weak at the knees. 'Don't worry about it,' he murmured, 'I'm not. Where's he going to sleep?'

'Er—well, I thought the fourth bedroom, if we could tidy it up a bit . . .'

'Stick him in the room Paul uses. There's a washbasin and a shaving point in there. That would be best, don't you think?'

'Yes, great. Thanks, Simon.'

'Any time.' He stroked her cheek lightly with the back of his hand and disappeared into his own room.

Vicky shoved her own cases through into her bedroom, then hung over the banister rail to wait for Tim's return. Simon was being extraordinarily agreeable, she mused. It didn't seem to bother him that she was entertaining so soon, and a male friend at that. Which must mean that he didn't have the slightest interest in her as a woman, mustn't it? Coming to that conclusion left her feeling as deflated as she had felt high a moment ago.

'Tim! Up here,' she called when he reappeared. 'Simon's brother is away at the moment, so you're not putting anybody out,' she explained, after showing him where he was to sleep. 'Anything you need, just ask. The bathroom's over here . . . I'll find you some towels.'

Having washed and changed, Vicky set off with Tim in search of their evening meal. The sun was a ball of flame in the west. Tim was in high spirits driving through the narrow, winding lanes to find the fifteenth-century inn which she had in mind. At times he exclaimed about the tracts of damaged woodlands they passed, where great trees still lay uprooted and slender birches were snapped off mid-trunk, the aftermath of the freak hurricane the previous autumn.

'That was some gale they had here last October,' he observed.

'Yes,' Vicky agreed, 'my aunt wrote to tell me about it at the time, but I never dreamed it was anything like as bad as this. It'll be years before it's all cleared up.'

She felt strangely doleful. Seeing the desolation of parts of the lovely countryside she had known added to her sober mood. Much as she had looked forward to Tim's visit, she could have wished him anywhere but where he was at this particular time. Where she really would have liked to be was back at the house, unpacking properly, pottering about, perhaps having another informal meal with Simon. She found herself wondering if he'd eaten properly that day, or whether he'd existed on sandwiches. He might have skipped lunch altogether if his clinic had been that busy.

They'd seen no more of the doctor before they left the house, but when Vicky had gone into her bedroom to change, on the dressing table she had found a stem vase with a single pink rose in it. Cut from the garden that morning, obviously. And underneath the vase, scrawled across one of Simon's visiting cards, was the word *Welcome.*

Oh, Simon! Do you really mean that? she had thought, a catch in her throat. He was not really the sort of person to say or do things which he didn't mean. All right, so he was going out of his way to be agreeable, it would be stupid to read anything more into a friendly gesture, she told herself firmly.

With an effort she roused herself to match her companion's holiday mood. They were nearing Penshurst when she saw the place she was looking for, an ancient rambling weatherboarded inn. Its window-boxes were bright with geraniums and there were hanging baskets crammed with trailing flowers. 'Here we are, Tim,' she said cheerfully, 'this has been standing here for five hundred years. How about that?'

'Strewth!' exclaimed Tim, pulling into the small adjoining parking area, 'I hope their hygiene's kept abreast of the times.'

Vicky giggled. 'Yes, you won't find sawdust on the floor, and they have a good menu as a rule. Come and see.'

Together they studied the handwritten bill of fare in its polished brass frame before going into the low-ceilinged bar for a pre-dinner drink.

They had reached the coffee stage when Tim asked, 'Who did you last come here with?'

'My parents, actually. It was my father's last birthday.' She fell silent, remembering. It had been winter then, a Sunday lunchtime affair, and there had been a glowing log fire in the huge fireplace, not a potted hydrangea as now. Chris had not been with them at the time. He had been playing rugby for his college.

Tim put out a hand and laid it over hers, seeing her pensive expression. 'Sorry—I didn't mean to stir up the past.'

She switched on a smile. 'Oh, it's all right. It's a pleasant memory really. It had snowed the night before and everywhere looked beautiful.'

His hand was still resting over hers. 'Vicky, I want to make you happy. Come back and marry me.'

Her eyes widened. She swallowed and laughed, choosing not to take him seriously. 'But I am happy, Tim, and I'm certainly not in a marrying mood, you'll probably be relieved to hear, knowing you. Come on, finish your coffee. It's still light enough for us to go and look at Chiddingstone. That's one of the most perfect Elizabethan villages you'll ever see.'

Tim gave her a one-sided smile and shook his head. 'My mother said I should never have let you get away!'

The next day, as planned, they visited the hop farm. Tim took Vicky's picture many times against the white-capped oasthouses and alongside the magnificent shire horses which were trained and cared for at the farm. Then there was a day in London, seeing as much as could be fitted in and ending with a trip to the theatre for the musical *Cats*.

Tim's last day they spent in a more leisurely fashion, swimming at the open-air pool and taking a riverside walk along the rural banks of the Medway. Vicky cooked for them at home that evening—grilled fillet steaks with mushrooms and broccoli, followed by an ice-cream gateau. There would have been enough of everything for Simon as well, but he didn't show up, much to her disappointment.

In fact, they had scarcely laid eyes on Simon since that first night of Tim's arrival. She wondered whether he had deliberately made himself scarce to be obliging, and she wished he hadn't. It was becoming increasingly difficult to keep things platonic between Tim and herself.

'Your mate never did get around to showing me your hospital,' Tim said, drying up for her after the meal. 'Perhaps we can fit it in when I come back.'

'Oh, will you be coming back this way?' Vicky queried.

'I can do, since it's en route for Heathrow. And I can't go back home without getting something sorted, Vicky. While I'm away, will you seriously think about what I said the other night . . . about coming back to Oz, even if you don't want to marry me—yet? Give us a chance.' He put an arm around her waist and kissed her cheek since she did not turn to face him. 'The idea might grow on you.'

'Oh, Tim,' she hesitated, embarrassed and not

wanting to hurt him, 'I-I've really enjoyed seeing you, but . . .'

He gave her a hug. 'OK, let's not spoil our last evening. We'll leave it open for the time being.'

The telephone ringing relieved the tension, but before she could reach the hall to answer it Simon had come in through the front door and picked up the receiver.

He waved to Vicky to indicate that the call was for him. 'Leah! Hallo, how are you?' Vicky heard him say, and for a moment she felt an irrational dislike for this shadowy girl who seemed to figure somewhere in Simon's life.

Going back into the kitchen where Tim was propped against the table, idly glancing through the morning paper, she said: 'Why don't you take that into the lounge, Tim? Simon's back. I'll make coffee.'

'OK, sweetheart, then I'll have to get my gear together. I'm catching a ferry from Dover in the morning, so I'd like to leave here by seven at the latest.'

He wandered off into the hall and she heard the agreeable rumble of male voices interspersed with pleasant laughter. Filling the coffee pot, she waited impatiently for the coffee to brew and sighed heavily, feeling thoroughly disconsolate.

It wasn't because Tim was leaving. If she were truthful, she was glad about that. And Simon was back again. And there was no earthly reason for her to feel put out because he was talking to a girl named Leah. She slammed a cupboard door after putting the coffee tin away.

'Steady on, you don't need to put all that beef behind it!' Simon remarked, coming in and looking quite pleased with life.

'Hi!' returned Vicky. 'I thought you'd abandoned me.'

He laughed, a low delicious sound which had her toes curling. 'You missed me?'

'Only in so far as I wanted to thank you for the rose and the welcome. It almost came down to leaving a note on your pillow. But you wouldn't have seen it. You haven't been here,' she said, trying and failing to sound indifferent.

'No. Sorry if that worried you. My new SHO seemed to be floundering, so I decided to stay at the hospital in case of need. But I don't think you'll have any trouble with this one,' Simon went on, 'he's a very earnest sort of guy. His mind is totally on the job.'

'Good, although personally I had no trouble with Adrian,' Vicky said lightly. 'Coffee?'

'Yes, please.' Hands in the pockets of his well-tailored grey trousers, Simon lounged against a worktop, his attentive eyes following her every movement. 'And have you had a good time with your friend?' he equired after a moment.

'Terrific. The time has simply flown. He has to leave early in the morning, and I'm on duty at one, so after that you'll have the whole place to yourself for the rest of the day.' She gave him a cheeky sideways grin. 'Won't that be nice for you?'

'Well, it is nice to come home,' he admitted,

'even if I do get called in again. Get this weekend over and perhaps we can settle down to some kind of normality.'

'Mmm,' she murmured, concentrating on putting cups and saucers, milk and coffee pot on a tray. 'Are you coming in to have this with us?'

'Is that all right—or would you rather be alone?'

'Of course not. For Pete's sake, we're just friends,' Vicky laughed, 'and I'm quite sure Tim would enjoy talking to you. He was saying just now that he would have liked to see the hospital.'

'OK, so long as I'm not intruding . . .' Simon picked up the tray and she followed his broad-shouldered upright figure into the lounge.

After setting the tray down on the low coffee table, Simon made himself comfortable in one of the deep armchairs.

Tim, occupying most of the settee, moved over to make room for Vicky and, when she had poured the drinks, she sat down beside him.

'Tell Simon about your new job, Tim,' she encouraged, to set the conversation rolling . . .

Early the following morning Vicky awoke with a start to the sound of her alarm clock ringing. Quickly she stretched out a hand to silence it, not wanting to disturb Simon. Yawning and stretching for a moment, she then slipped out of bed, pulled on her dressing-gown and padded across the landing to arouse Tim.

The previous night the three of them had stayed talking into the small hours, discussing the different approaches to health care in their respective countries, and now Tim was sleeping soundly. She had to shake him a couple of times before he grunted and turned over.

'Tim! Come on, Tim!' she urged in a fierce whisper. 'It's gone six o'clock, and if you want to catch that ferry . . .'

He grunted again and suddenly reached up and grabbed her.

Losing her balance, Vicky collapsed on top of him. 'Sh!' she warned, giggling. 'Stop messing about—you'll wake Simon!'

'Oh, blow Simon!' Tim exclaimed. 'I was having a fantastic dream about you just now, and then there you were in my arms.'

She stifled another giggle. 'Who are you kidding? Look, I'll just nip into the bathroom first, and then I'll go down and make you some breakfast. Don't go to sleep again, will you, or I'll come in with a cold flannel.'

'That sounds more like my luck,' Tim groaned. 'Think I'll go back and finish my dream.'

'You haven't got time,' Vicky said. 'I'll only be five minutes.'

After a quick rinse, she pulled on a primrose jog suit and went downstairs. Tim joined her presently and they sat together in the kitchen, talking quietly, while he breakfasted on toast and coffee.

'Pity you can't come with me,' Tim said.

'Yes, it should be a lovely day for a Channel crossing.'

'You going back to bed when I've gone?'

'That was the general idea,' Vicky said, 'although it seems pointless now I'm up. I might just potter.'

'Well, I shall think of you while I'm away. And I'll be back, remember,' warned Tim, wagging a finger at her. 'I wasn't joshing, you know, about you coming back to Oz.'

She picked up his empty dishes and dumped them in the sink before turning to smile at him. 'Thanks for the compliment, Tim. But I haven't got England out of my system yet.'

'So long as it's only England,' he muttered. Getting up from the table, he came towards her. 'Do I get a kiss goodbye?'

'Of course you do,' she returned, arms outstretched.

But the hugging and the kissing left her with a feeling of nothing more than friendly warmth. Oh yes, she felt affection for him, but there was no mystical tingle, no army of butterflies in her stomach, and no awful sadness to think that he was leaving. Whatever she felt for Tim, there was no passion in it. He simply failed to arouse her whatever in that way.

Opening the front door, Vicky waited for Tim to pick up his travel bag, then followed him out to the driveway. There they both paused as Tim exclaimed, 'Oh dear!' and Vicky clapped a hand to her mouth. Simon's car was parked behind Tim's, effectively blocking his exit.

'Perhaps I could move it. Do you know where his keys are?' Tim murmured.

'Not the slightest idea,' Vicky said. 'In his room,

most likely, but we can have a look downstairs.'

A quick search brought no success, so there was nothing for it but to wake the doctor.

Vicky ran upstairs and tapped on his closed door, calling, 'Simon!'

'Yes?' he answered. 'Come in.'

With an apology on her lips and a clamour in her breast, she looked in. Much to her relief she found him propped up in bed reading. 'Sorry to disturb you, Simon, but your car's parked behind Tim's. I-If you'd like to let me have your keys, he could move it . . .'

'Oh! OK, I'd better do it myself,' he said in a patient tone of voice. 'Be with you in a jiff.'

Moments later he skimmed down the stairs, clad in jeans and sweatshirt, unshaven, his fair hair tousled. Waving aside their further apologies, he quickly backed the BMW and waited for Tim to zoom off before returning his own car to the drive.

Vicky stayed waving to Tim until he turned the corner and was lost to sight. She found Simon waiting for her in the drive.

'It's a good thing I'm used to dressing in a hurry, isn't it?' he remarked conversationally, draping an arm around her shoulders as they went back to the house together.

She smiled up at him, her senses thrilling to his touch. 'Yes—a pity we had to disturb you, though. Are you always awake early?'

'Providing I haven't been up half the night. I like to jog in the mornings, when I can. I find that invigorating. God's in his heaven, all's right with the world, sort of stuff. How about you, are you a morning girl or a night bird?' Simon enquired.

'I'm both—I have to be. But I shan't ever be joining you on a jog. When I'm on a late I usually like to have a lie-in.' Vicky felt an odd sense of loss when he took his arm from her shoulders. 'No point in going back to bed now, though. I'm wide awake.'

Simon's candid blue eyes were searching hers. 'You look a bit sad,' he said.

She felt herself flush, and laughed, hoping he hadn't read her thoughts. 'I'm not. I've no reason to be.'

He passed a hand thoughtfully over his chin. 'I just wondered. Are you in love with that fellow?'

Vicky smiled in relief. 'Tim? I like him. I like him a lot, but that's as far as it goes. Why?'

'Because it effects me, doesn't it? I mean, if you *were* in love with him, you might be thinking of shooting back to Australia.'

She drew a deep breath and let it out with emphasis. 'Well, I can assure you I'm not . . . and I'm not,' she said edgily.

Simon waved a peaceable hand. 'All right, all right. Just checking. I wondered if I might be having to get a move on over certain matters,' he said with irritating composure. 'Give me a minute to run a razor over my stubble and we'll celebrate our partnership by breakfasting together. I'll demonstrate my prowess at boiling eggs.' Whistling cheerfully, he took the stairs two at a time, leaving Vicky gazing after him, pushing her hair back in utter bewilderment.

Why was he so pleased to hear she was not involved with Tim? At first, when Simon had left them the run of the house she had wondered whether it was out of discretion, or because he hoped that an affair might be developing and she would be encouraged to return to Sydney. Now, apparently, he was glad that Tim's visit had not changed things. Was that because he felt he needed more time to persuade her to sell him the house?

What really puzzled her was why this particular house was so special. True, it was convenient for the hospital, and certainly less trouble to stay there than to move. But that said, it wouldn't be impossible to find somewhere else. Now that she had agreed to come and share it with him she was beginning to feel it was a mistake. If he had only to touch her to fire her senses (or even to turn his eyes on her for that matter), it was going to take plenty of willpower to keep a cool head.

She found herself thinking of Beryl and appreciating the kind of power that Adrian had wielded over her. At all costs, Vicky determined, she would not let herself get caught in that kind of web. She had a mind of her own, hadn't she? It was a question of exercising control and not letting physical inclinations get the better of you.

In any case, sooner or later the arrangement was bound to come to an end. Simon would decide to get married, or he could move from the area. Personally she was happy to be a free agent. She had no wish to get deeply involved with anyone for the time being. Therefore there really was no reason why she and

Simon couldn't share happily for as long as it suited them. While he was willing she decided she would do her utmost to make it work.

CHAPTER NINE

SIMON'S hasty grooming took him scarcely any time. Vicky, having reset the table, was debating what to do next when she heard him coming downstairs again.

Chin smooth-shaven, bright hair brushed and settling into its rich, careless waves, 'How's that?' he demanded, presenting himself for inspection.

Eyeing his strong profile, she returned jokingly, 'Fantastic! But you don't have to go to these lengths on my account, Simon. You're entitled to be a slob at home if you want to be.'

'I never treat a lady to designer stubble for breakfast if I can help it,' he declared, crossing to where she stood by the fridge.

'Oh! You often make breakfast for ladies, do you?'

'Maybe *often* is a slight exaggeration. Now, would you like to move yourself, madam, and let the expert take over?' With a hand on either side of her waist, he pushed her towards a chair and sat her down. 'How do you like your eggs—soft, hard, or indifferent?'

'Soft yolk, solid white, please. If you can manage that.' She wasn't really hungry, but she thought it would do no harm to humour him. Still savouring the warm, subtle tang of his skin as they had passed, she rested her chin on her hands and watched him get to work.

With Tim's unexpected arrival on the doorstep earlier that week, she had spent little time in the house so far, and this morning was virtually the start of her link-up with Simon. She was determined to do her best to make it work, even if it did seem unbelievable that she was there at all.

'I'm not used to being waited on,' she said presently. 'Can't I do anything?'

'Now she asks me!' Simon flashed her a wicked grin and set toast on the table. 'Make the most of it while I'm in the mood. This is probably a one-off.'

She grinned back. 'I'm sure there must be a catch in it somewhere.'

'My word, you have got a suspicious nature! Here's me doing my best to make a good impression and that's all the thanks I get!'

Vicky ducked and laughed as he flicked a drop of water in her direction. If this was his idea of getting back to normal, then she loved it.

They had much to talk about, and had they not been interrupted some time later by the ringing telephone, she wondered how long they might have lingered over their meal.

'How would you rather we split things?' she asked. 'Would you like to have either the lounge or the dining-room for your own use, or . . .?'

'Good heavens, no. Unless you'd prefer it. There's the study when I've any writing or research to do. Why don't we just share the whole place? We can always come to a mutual agreement if either of us needs some privacy for any reason.'

In spite of her intentions to keep a firm check on any wayward flights of fancy, Vicky soon felt cocooned in a rosy glow of pleasure. It was fascinating to be there, listening to the cadence of the doctor's deep voice, exchanging views with him on things other than their work, watching his discerning, expressive face as he talked.

She was rapidly being charmed, and she was aware of it. And she found she didn't care that it was only the house which had brought them together. As Anna had pointed out, Simon must find her company agreeable or he would never have suggested the arrangement.

They were discussing the idea that they might give a dinner party and invite the new SHO, amongst others, when Simon was called to the hospital.

'We'll get back to that later,' he said, 'although *when* remains to be seen. Stick a note up somewhere of when you're on or off duty. That might help.'

After he had gone Vicky idled through the rest of her morning off feeling unaccountably blissful. She finished her unpacking at last, then washed her hair, then picked a bunch of asters from the garden and put them in a cut glass vase on the hall table. And every now and then she found herself bursting into song. Exactly why she should feel so chuffed she didn't know. And how long this agreeable state of affairs would last was another matter. So long as Simon was prepared to let it, she supposed. Nothing had really changed between them. In reality there was only one sensible thing to do—enjoy it while it lasted and let the future take care of itself.

There was another phone call for Simon just before Vicky was about to set off for work at midday.

'Is Dr Drummond there?' a female voice enquired.

'No, he's at the hospital,' Vicky returned. 'Can I take a message?'

'Er—well, just tell him Leah rang,' the voice answered, 'and I'll ring again later.'

Vicky scribbled the message on the telephone pad. As she cycled along to the hospital her outlook was not quite so rose-coloured as before that phone call. When Simon's brother had mentioned Leah he seemed to suggest that she had been an embarrassment to Simon. Leah, whoever she was, had also telephoned the previous evening. Whatever had gone on between them, it obviously wasn't yet over.

After lunching in the hospital canteen, Vicky reported to Coco Ward at one o'clock. She found a happy atmosphere prevailing that Saturday afternoon. It was one of those days when they were seeing a good outcome for some of their efforts.

To begin with, a satisfactory X-ray of his fractured femur had at last cleared seven-year-old Shaun—the boy from Canberra—for the journey home. There was still work to be done on his wasted leg muscles, but no reason why he should not travel. Once over the initial trauma he had been a delightful child to nurse, and all the staff had grown fond of Shaun and his mother.

Now, coming into the office to say goodbye, his mother left them with a parting gift of a large box of chocolates. 'You've all been terrific,' she said. 'We'll never forget you, will we, Shaun?'

'No, but I can't wait to see my dad again,' he declared.

His physiotherapist laughed. 'And I bet your mum seconds that! Now you go carefully, will you? No playing football yet awhile.'

After hugs and kisses all round Vicky accompanied mother and son to the ward door to see them off. There had been a special bond between the three of them, with Vicky having recently worked in Australia, and she felt a pang of nostalgia at seeing them go.

'Give my love to Oz,' she said.

Mrs Darby smiled and kissed her again. 'Listen, if ever you come back, promise you'll come and see us? I really mean that. You've got our address on his papers, haven't you?'

'Yes, and I will, if I ever do,' Vicky promised, although not believing that she ever would.

Another happy child that day was Lisa. Her temperature had been stable for some time, her white cell count was down, and her latest X-ray showed a healthy callous forming where the bone abscess had been excised. Although not yet permitted to bear weight on her leg, she was mobile in a wheelchair and able to visit and play with other children. Helping her back to bed for her afternoon rest, Vicky learned what else was making Lisa so cheerful.

'Mummy and Daddy are going to get married

again,' she confided, 'but they're going to wait till my leg's really better—so I can be a bridesmaid.'

'Oh, Lisa, that's great, isn't it? How exciting!' Vicky gave the little girl a swift hug. 'Well, you drink up all your juice and eat up your meals and you'll be as fit as Wonder Woman in no time.'

As always at weekends, there was much coming and going on the ward. More visitors arrived than on weekdays, some patients were being discharged and new waiting-list patients admitted. Sister Lorne being off duty, Beryl had been in overall charge since early morning. Responsibility suited her and she seemed in good heart despite her recent agonising over Adrian.

There had been no doctors on the ward since Vicky's arrival that afternoon. She had wondered whether they might see Simon since he'd been called in, but when Beryl handed over to her at four o'clock they had seen nothing of him or his houseman.

'What do you think of Simon's new sidekick?' asked Vicky, pinning the ward keys into her own pocket.

'Mark Jones?' Beryl gave a slight smile. 'He's not bad, although he's a bit of a clown. Wears a clingy bear on his stethoscope. And he did a head-over-heels in the playroom yesterday because one of the kids betted him he couldn't.'

Vicky laughed. 'Determined to get down to their level, is he? At least he doesn't sound toffee-nosed.'

Beryl agreed. 'He's certainly not a womaniser,' she

added. 'If you batted your eyes at him he'd probably think you'd got dust in them.'

They both giggled, and Vicky said, 'Well, it makes life less complicated if he keeps his mind on the job.'

Soon after Beryl had left the ward, the new SHO walked in, a stocky young man with cropped brown hair, straight dark eyebrows and an intent expression.

'Er—good afternoon,' he said, coming into the office where Vicky was filling in diet sheets for the next day. Acknowledging a strange face, he introduced himself. 'I'm Mark Jones, on Sir James Latimer's firm.'

'Hello, Mark,' Vicky returned. 'I did recognise you—I heard about the bear,' she smiled.

The clingy bear was now on the lapel of his white coat. Mark glanced at it, solemn-faced. 'Oh, this. Well, you have to try and disarm the opposition somehow, don't you?'

'The opposition?' laughed Vicky. 'You mean the kids. Yes, it can be a tough assignment sometimes, but we don't have any problems here at the moment. What can I do for you?'

'Ah, well,' he said looking at the case-notes folder in his hands, 'I'd like to take some blood from Holly Marsh—we don't appear to have had a test since she came off the IV.'

Vicky frowned. 'We don't have a Holly Marsh here. Perhaps she's in Medical, across the corridor?'

He clapped a hand to his forehead. 'Sorry, my mistake—should have turned right instead of left.

Still finding my way around.'

He walked off back the way he had come, leaving Vicky slightly nonplussed but seeing what Beryl meant. The nursing staff were hardly likely to be pestered by this newcomer. He saw a uniform, which to him added up to information and assistance, and that was all.

Remaining on duty with Vicky after the early shift left were June, Marion and an eager second-year student nurse named Amanda. It was the usual hectic programme after suppers were over, seeing to washings and mouth care, in addition to the many clinical procedures, before their twenty young patients could be settled for the night. Those parents who were able to stay were glad to help with caring for their own children, which relieved some of the pressure on the staff. Not all parents, however, could stay, and there were sometimes tearful youngsters to be consoled when they left.

Eight-year-old Sally's mother was in tears herself as her daughter clung to her, weeping.

Seeing the mother's dilemma, Vicky went to ease the situation. The child was still feeling low after surgery three days ago to correct a malformation of one of her ureters. It had been a relief to them all to find there was no malignancy of the kidney involved.

Stroking Sally's hair, Vicky said gently, 'Mummy will come again as soon as she can, pet. But she has to go home sometimes, doesn't she? There's your brother and sister to look after. Mandy and I are going to give you a nice wash in a minute and then she'll read you a story. How about that?'

The little girl nodded tearfully, her bottom lip still tremulous, and outside the cubicle Mrs White paused, wanting reassurance.

'She is all right, isn't she, Nurse? I've never know her so droopy.'

'Yes, she's making good progress, Mrs White,' Vicky was glad to be able to say, 'but it's been a big ordeal and she's only a little girl. She's been very brave. It's understandable she should cry sometimes. She'll be getting a sedative presently. Try not to worry, we'll look after her. You'll find every day will make a big difference.'

True to her word, Vicky enlisted Amanda's help and they blanket-bathed Sally and made her comfortable for the night.

'There you are,' said Vicky, placing a pillow comfortably when they had finished, 'and tomorrow you may be able to get up for a while, now your drain is out and you're off the drip. That'll be nice, won't it? Like a story now?'

The little girl had brightened considerably during the nurses' attentions. 'Yes, please. Could I have my Famous Five book? Ooh, where's my bunny got to?' she queried, searching around for it.

'This old thing, do you mean?' Amanda picked up the shabby soft toy from the top of the locker and dangled it by its ears.

Vicky tutted. 'Mandy! What do you mean—*old thing*? He's a very important rabbit, isn't he Sal?' She patted the toy fondly before handing it over. 'He's as old as you, so your mummy told me.'

Satisfied that they had managed to bring a smile to the youngster's face, she wheeled away the washing trolley, leaving Amanda to renew childhood acquaintance with the Famous Five. Having been fully occupied with ward matters for the past few hours, personal affairs had been pushed to the back of Vicky's mind. With the arrival of the night staff, she handed over to Hazel Fisher and went off duty talking to June, who was about to go into her last study block before the Finals.

June said, with a sigh, 'I'm glad my stint on Coco is over. Sick kids really get to me.'

'Oh, come on, it's been nice today,' returned Vicky cheerfully. 'No heartbreakers.'

'No! And someone has to do it, I suppose. Good thing we don't all feel the same.' June gave her senior an appreciative smile. 'Coming over to the Swan for a drink?'

Vicky hesitated before answering. 'We-ell, not tonight, if you don't mind, June, I'm on an early tomorrow, and I'm not living in now. I've got a cycle ride ahead of me.'

'Oh, OK,' June answered amiably. See you around.'

They parted company and Vicky made for the locker room. After changing her uniform for civvies, she collected her bicycle from where it was padlocked and set off towards her old home.

The night breeze lifted her hair as she bowled along the country roads. The air was fragrant and invigorating after the confines of the hospital, and although her limbs were tired her heart was light.

She wondered, with an inner quiver of expectation, whether Simon would be there and, if so, whether they might resume their morning chat.

By the time she reached home it was ten p.m. The house was in total darkness and the doctor's car nowhere in evidence. Vicky was disappointed, much as she was loath to admit it. Well, it was the weekend, she reminded herself. Of course he was out. Even if he wasn't working he was hardly likely to be sitting at home twiddling his thumbs waiting for her! In any case, it was no concern of hers where he was.

Putting her bicycle away in the empty garage, she let herself into the house, quickly switching on lights everywhere to banish the gloom. She began to wish she had gone out with June after all. She felt jumpy. She didn't like dark rooms and pools of shadow, although it had never bothered her until the family tragedy. Now the ghosts began crowding in at night if she was alone, but she obviously couldn't count on Simon's company. Solitude was something she would have to learn to cope with if she were to stay here.

For company Vicky turned on the television set in the lounge. She was greeted by a weatherman forecasting the end of the fine spell of weather, but the friendly voice was welcome despite his prophecy of storms ahead. Leaving the set running, she went upstairs, switching on more lights before changing her clothes for bed. Then, wrapping her turquoise silk happi-coat over her fun-print cotton nightshirt, she wandered downstairs again for a bedtime snack, leaving all the lights blazing.

After making herself a cream cheese sandwich and a coffee, Vicky curled up on the sofa in front of the television to watch the late-night chat show. It only half held her interest. Her thoughts kept straying, mostly in the direction of Simon. She couldn't help wondering where he was, and if he would be home at all that night. Perhaps he was out with that girl Leah? The idea set a little grub of envy gnawing away at her heart.

It was after eleven when she heard the sounds of a car arriving, then the garage doors being closed. Vicky's spirits soared. Simon was home! He was home! Excitement sang through her veins, thinking of his strong, dynamic presence. She felt ridiculously glad.

Had they been lovers, she knew she would have been jumping off the sofa and dashing out to greet him. To be held in a close embrace against his powerful body would have been worth all the waiting. But they were not lovers. And Simon didn't know she was in love with him. So she stayed quietly where she was, scarcely able to breathe, listening for his key in the front door.

Oh God, this was so stupid! It was going to be impossible to live here if this was how he was going to affect her. She would be laying up enormous problems for herself unless she kept her head. That day in his aunt's garden she had known that here was a man who could sweep the feet from under her. It was madness to have allowed it to happen.

The front door clicked open and shut. Vicky's

heart drummed and her mouth dried. Would he come in to say goodnight? He might have brought someone back with him. He might simply call out to her—or perhaps she ought to check that it really *was* Simon? Questions shot through her mind in rapid succession. She drew a number of deep breaths, trying to keep calm.

Simon himself solved her problem by tapping lightly on the half-open door of the room and looking in. 'Oh, there you are,' he said levelly. 'All alone? May I come in?'

Vicky threw him a pleased, half-anxious smile. 'Hello, Simon. Yes, come in. I'm not really watching this—just unwinding before bed.' Pressing the remote control, she switched off the television programme and turned to look at him.

Elegant and irresistibly attractive in formal black dinner jacket, he paused on the threshold before joining her. 'I didn't know which room you were in. There are lights all over the place.'

'Well, it was pitch black when I got back. It felt spooky,' she said lamely, 'a-and I didn't know whether you'd be home tonight or not.'

'Ah!' The doctor scratched his cheek thoughtfully. 'It didn't occur to me to leave a light on. Sorry about that. I will another time.' His sudden, endearing smile fired her with longing as, removing his jacket, he threw it over the back of a chair and came to sit opposite her, resting his hands lightly between his knees. 'Did I scare you when I came in?' His deep blue eyes searched hers. 'You looked about to jump out of your skin!'

Vicky half smiled and tightened the belt of her wrap. 'Yes and no. I'm not yet used to this kind of set-up—men rolling in and out of the house at all hours.' She looked him over appreciatively. 'Have you been somewhere nice?'

'More interesting than nice.' Simon took off his bow tie and undid the neck button of his white evening shirt. 'I had dinner with Sir James and a few of his buddies, followed by some rather heavyweight discussion, about lasers.'

He leaned back in the chair, long legs outstretched, hands clasped behind his head, watching her. Vicky sat with one foot tucked beneath her, the other bare leg outstretched along the sofa. He didn't want to talk about medical matters now. Her appealing vulnerability was making powerful inroads into his psyche. He sensed the need to play this carefully. It wouldn't do to jump the gun before she was ready.

'And what have you been doing with yourself?' he asked. 'Taking good care of my patients?'

'Taking good care of *our* patients,' she corrected. 'Actually, we said goodbye to Shaun today. I got invited to visit them, if ever I go back to Australia.'

'Did you indeed? There's someone else who'd rather like to know whether that's on the cards,' Simon murmured.

She was not quite sure whether he meant Tim or himself, so she let it pass. 'I left you a message, about Leah phoning. Did you find it?'

'Yes, thanks, I did.'

'Who is she?' Vicky hadn't intended to ask. It slipped out before she could stop herself.

'Why do you want to know?'

She shrugged carelessly. 'Just feminine curiosity.' It didn't help that he looked amused. Shifting her position slightly, she tucked both feet further under her. 'That morning your brother found me here,' she said, 'he thought at first I was her. Are we alike?'

Simon leaned forward again and studied her from every angle. 'Like Leah? Rubbish! Not a bit, except that you're both small and dark. What else did my little brother say?'

'Nothing. He said I'd better ask you. I just wondered how she liked her eggs cooked,' Vicky retorted.

Simon threw back his head and laughed. 'And now you're none the wiser, are you?'

'No.'

'Well, my dear Victoria, to save my character from complete assassination, I'll tell you the story. Paul is a well-intentioned but misguided clot, and Leah is a very nubile seventeen-year-old. He picked her up one night, thumbing a lift on the London Road. She'd left home because her stepfather beat her up, and she'd run out of money. Paul didn't like to abandon her, so he brought her here.' Simon ran a hand through his hair despairingly.

Vicky frowned. 'Oh! Was that a tall story—or was she genuine?'

'Yes, she was genuine all right. But you'll appreciate my position. A doctor has to be careful of nubile young women. A pity you weren't living here at the time.'

She couldn't help a wry laugh. 'I see. So you

don't feel compromised by me?'

He looked at her askance. 'Don't be provocative! You know what I mean. I couldn't let her stay here, could I? Anyway, after a bit of straight talking about the dangers of thumbing lifts from strange young men, we decided to rope in Aunt Vinny. She gave Leah a bed for a couple of nights. She also found her a job and a bed-sit, via her many contacts. That was six months ago. Now Leah is going to join her natural father in Canada and she was ringing to tell me the good news. End of story. And you're much prettier,' he added.

Vicky smiled and was silent for a moment. She imagined there was far more to the story than this bald statement of facts. She could picture Simon, his face stern, berating the girl for hitch-hiking, and Paul for picking her up. 'Lucky Leah,' she murmured, 'meeting with the Drummond brothers instead of a pair of villains.'

'Said with your hand on your heart?'

'But of course—ouch!' Vicky exclaimed, suddenly clutching the back of her thigh. 'I've got cramp.' She straightened her legs from under her and stood up, flexing her knee back and forth. But the spasm got worse, her hamstrings tightening painfully.

'Well, if you must try being a contortionist, what else can you expect?' Simon remarked unfeelingly.

'Thanks. You're a great help!' winced Vicky, hobbling painfully about while rubbing the back of her leg. The torsion didn't ease. She dropped to the floor in agony, hugging her knees, biting her lip to stop from crying.

Realising she needed help, Simon got down beside her. 'That's not the way. Extend your leg, and press right down. Come on, right down. Reflex action—one set of muscles working against the other. Didn't you learn that in An and Phys?' With skilful hands he exerted pressure over her knee joint until the seizure finally eased.

She sighed with relief. 'Oh—that's better. Thanks. That was awful, for a moment.'

'OK now?'

She nodded. With his hands still touching her she couldn't trust herself to speak.

He helped her up and held her to him while massaging the back of her leg to complete the cure. 'You're out of condition, my girl. Too much lying around on Australian beaches.'

Making the effort to retaliate, Vicky said: 'Do you mind? Haven't I just cycled to the hospital and back?'

'As I said. You must be out of condition. You'll have to come jogging with me some time.'

'All right, and you can let me go now. I shan't fall down.'

'Supposing I don't?' said Simon, clasping her even more firmly to him. 'What could you do about it?'

It was heaven and it was hell to be in his arms like this. Her body cried out to be loved. But he was playing games, while she was gradually losing the battle for restraint. 'Don't underrate my fragile strength,' she warned with an attempt at humour.

Simon groaned. 'Oh, Vicky . . . stop babbling and kiss me, you adorable armful!'

He gave her no opportunity to refuse. His mouth came down over hers, gently at first, then increasingly demanding. She made a feeble attempt to push him away, but his ardour overwhelmed her and soon they were locked together in a passionate embrace.

Vicky's head swam. Was this the cool, controlled Dr Drummond? He seemed as suffused with desire as she was herself. Could it be that he was really in love with her? Or was it the beast within that Aunt Celia had talked about? At that moment it didn't seem to matter. She was in his arms, where she had longed to be, and his actions suggested that he felt the same.

As they kissed he caressed her tenderly, giving her exquisite joy. Of their own volition her arms encircled his neck while her body moulded to his. All her reserves melted. She felt like a flower opening to the sun which probed her innermost depths.

It came as a momentous shock when, presently, Simon held her a little away and, looking into her eyes, began thickly, 'Vicky, my darling, about this house . . .'

The world tumbled about her ears. She should have known that was all he wanted—all he had ever wanted. How could she have been such a fool as to think otherwise?

'Oh, have the wretched thing!' she snapped, cutting him off in mid-sentence. 'I'll go back to Australia. You'd like that, wouldn't you? It'll get me off your conscience . . .'

Looking startled, he gave her a slight shake.

'Vicky, just a minute . . .'

'What's so special about this place anyway?' she flared.

'I'll tell you, if you'll let me get a word in.'

'Anyone'd think you'd struck gold in the garden. Let me *go*!' She pummelled on his chest, trying to push him off, but he would have none of it.

'Certainly not. I admit my timing seems to have gone adrift . . .'

'You can say that again! There was no need to pretend . . . to make love to me. You want the house, I've said you can have it . . . Now leave me alone!'

'Give me strength, woman!' Simon sighed, holding her even more firmly. 'It's not your damn house I want. It's you. *You.* YOU! Don't you understand? I've wanted you from the moment you scowled at me in the car-park that day.'

Vicky gazed at him with dawning wonder and her voice came out in an unrecognisable squeak. 'Me? But I thought . . .'

'Well, you thought wrong,' he growled. 'Do what you like with the place. My feeling for you has nothing to do with houses. I was merely about to say that I thought it would be best to let your cousin have it. I'm getting my consultancy when Sir James retires. I can put down permanent roots somewhere. And I'd prefer that to be somewhere that's got no sad links with your past, because I want you with me. I love you, Vicky—I love you desperately. Don't ever leave me, my darling.'

'Oh, Simon . . .' Her eyes misted over. She was half laughing, half crying now. The rest of what she wanted to say was cut short as his lips took hers, convincing her beyond all doubt of his sincerity.

Later, relaxing in each other's arms, they talked out the events of their coming together.

'My life was plain sailing until you exploded on to the scene,' Simon told her, between kisses. 'At first I'd decided I might as well try and buy this house instead of throwing money away on rent. But that was before I knew who you were. Afterwards, it complicated matters. The accident to your family made it a sensitive area. I didn't want to rush you. I wanted to give you time to sort yourself out. I wanted to court you properly—to make you fall in love with me. But love dictates its own timing . . .'

Vicky stroked his hair and pulled his face down to hers again. 'Darling, you didn't have to make me fall in love. I did. That's why I was in two minds about moving in here. I thought it was the house you wanted, not me.'

Simon grinned ruefully. 'It did vaguely cross my addled brain to wonder if that's what you would think. But I also thought if I could get you to come here to live it might get the place out of your system as well as giving you time to get to know me. Then up pops your Australian friend, and I had visions of you disappearing to the back of beyond again. My dearest, adorable Vicky, I'm besotted with you. Please marry me—like now, if not sooner?'

Her throat ached with love as her eyes misted over again. 'Yes, please,' she said, with a tremor in her voice. 'I was only waiting to be asked.' She laughed softly, looking up into his ardent face. 'I was madly jealous of Leah,' she admitted.

'And I could have throttled Tim. But do you know something?' Simon went on, dropping small sweet kisses on her upturned face. 'I really did strike gold, landing here. My only regret is that it took your loss, your pain to bring us together. Sadly, that's how it happens sometimes, sweetheart.'

Vicky nodded. 'Yes, but I'm not going to look back any more,' she resolved. 'As the poet pointed out, we ought to make the most of what we have while we have it. Oh, Simon, I do love you. Hold me.'

'For the rest of our lives, my darling.'

Had the sky fallen or the seas dried at that particular moment in time, Simon and Vicky would barely have noticed.

SANDRA CANFIELD
CHERISH
THIS
RISA KIRK
BEYOND
REDWOOD
EMPIRE

Mills & Boon

WINTER COMPETITION

How would you like a year's supply of Mills & Boon Romances ABSOLUTELY FREE? Well, you can win them! All you have to do is complete the word puzzle below and send it into us by 30th June 1989.
The first five correct entries picked out of the bag after that date will each win a year's supply of Mills & Boon Romances (Ten books every month - **worth over £100!**) What could be easier?

Ivy
Frost
Bleak
Boot
Robin
Yule
Freeze

Radiate
Chill
Glow
Ice
Hibernate
Icicle
Gloves

December
Skate
Mistletoe
Fire
Log
Scarf
Berry

Star
Ski
Inn

Merry
Pine

PLEASE TURN OVER FOR DETAILS ON HOW TO ENTER

How to enter

All the words listed overleaf, below the word puzzle, are hidden in the grid. You can find them by reading the letters forwards, backwards, up or down, or diagonally. When you find a word, circle it, or put a line through it. After you have found all the words the remaining letters (which you can read from left to right, from the top of the puzzle through to the bottom) will spell a secret message.

Don't forget to fill in your name and address in the space provided and pop this page in an envelope (you don't need a stamp) and post it today. Hurry - competition ends 30th June 1989

Only one entry per household please.

Mills & Boon Competition,
FREEPOST,
P.O. Box 236,
Croydon,
Surrey CR9 9EL.

Secret message ______________________________

____

Name ______________________________

Address ______________________________

____

____

______________________________ Postcode ______________

COMP5